Hot Alphas. Smart Women. Sexy Stories.

MAN IN
CHARGE

LAURELIN PAIGE

MAN IN
CHARGE

ALSO BY LAURELIN PAIGE

Visit my website for a more detailed reading order.

Man in Charge Duet
Man in Charge
Man in Love

The Dirty Universe
Dirty Filthy Rich Boys - READ FREE
Dirty Duet: Dirty Filthy Rich Men | Dirty Filthy Rich Love
Dirty Games Duet: Dirty Sexy Player | Dirty Sexy Games
Dirty Sweet Duet: Sweet Liar | Sweet Fate
Dirty Filthy Fix (a spinoff novella)
Dirty Wild Trilogy: Wild Rebel Coming 2021

The Fixed Universe
Fixed Series: Fixed on You | Found in You | Forever with You | Hudson | Fixed Forever
Found Duet: Free Me | Find Me
Chandler (a spinoff novel)
Falling Under You (a spinoff novella)
Dirty Filthy Fix (a spinoff novella)
Slay Series: Rivalry | Ruin | Revenge | Rising
The Open Door (a spinoff novella)
Slash (a Slay spinoff novella)

First and Last
First Touch | Last Kiss

Hollywood Standalones
One More Time
Close
Sex Symbol
Star Struck

Written with Sierra Simone
Porn Star | Hot Cop

Written with Kayti McGee under the name Laurelin McGee
Miss Match | Love Struck | MisTaken | Holiday for Hire

Dear Reader,

I'm excited to introduce you to my new world, the world of the Sebastians - a wealthy, powerful family with so many opportunities for angsty billionaire love stories. I hope to bring you more from them in the future, and this is the beginning.

If you have already been introduced to this world by reading my novella, *Man on Top*, please skip to Chapter Seven.

If you haven't read *Man on Top*, or you'd enjoy a refresher, turn the page and begin the book with Chapter One.

xoxo
Laurelin

For Lauren Blakely.

And because of Lauren Blakely.

When I said I had a story idea inspired by Working Girl but didn't have time to write it, she reminded me that I make my own schedule.

Oh, yeah. I do.

ONE

I was holding my phone up, looking for a signal when I heard it. A soft mewling. The kind of sound a kitten makes when it's in trouble.

Perking my ears, I scanned my surroundings. Behind me, four metal silo-shaped structures huddled together. Below me, the crowded rooftop bar pulsed with high energy. In front of me, the Empire State glowed prominently in rainbow colors (in honor of the LGBTQ rally happening that weekend), but the abundance of flashing club lights from the venue made the famous tourist site pale in comparison. It was loud too, which was part of the reason I'd snuck up the steel staircase to the building's highest level, wanting to make a phone call. The other reason being that I had yet to get more than one bar to show on my screen.

The mewling, I determined, had to be coming from the silos, whatever they were. I imagined they housed mechanical items for the building—electrical, air conditioning, whatnot. Some top-notch architect had for some reason decided that bronzed cylindrical towers with tops that

2 | LAURELIN PAIGE

looked like Asian rice hats was the best way to pretty up the industrial equipment. Seriously, trendy New York City design style was beyond my grasp. They were weird, as far as I was concerned.

And they were also on the top of a building with sixty stories, so the likelihood that I'd heard a lost cat was relatively slim.

The sound had stopped, anyway. It had probably been just a squeak of a generator, or I'd imagined it. I went back to my phone. Two bars now when I faced this direction. I climbed the remaining three steps to the official top level. Three bars! That would work.

Except, now I heard the cat again.

Twice more. It definitely wasn't mechanical. I lowered my phone and crept cautiously around one of the silos. If it wasn't a cat—which it couldn't be this high up, right?—then what was it? Did rats make those noises?

I cringed at the possibility. There was honestly no reason to look for the source.

But what if it *was* a cat? Maybe the hipster bar kept one up here to take care of the mice. It wasn't the most ridiculous idea, and my curiosity was piqued, so against my better instincts, I continued around the curve of the second silo.

Then I froze.

It wasn't an animal making those noises—it was a woman. She was about fifteen feet away, her back pressed against the brick wall that framed a smokestack on the other side of the silos. Her eyes were closed, her cocktail dress gathered up around her waist, and the sounds she was making were whimpers of pleasure, not distress. Probably due to the man standing in front of her. More specifically, his hand working between her legs.

And, wow, he was really working it if the expression on her face was any indication.

Quickly and quietly, I scuttled back around the silo and let out a slow breath. I didn't know if I should laugh or...well. What other reaction should I have? Certainly the instantaneous buzz of arousal between my thighs wasn't appropriate.

So laugh it was. A silent laugh, so as not to disturb the "lovers."

When the impulse at humor had passed, though, the buzz was still there. It had been way too long since I'd gotten laid. My last real relationship had ended the previous summer, then there'd been that one rebound hookup over the Halloween weekend, and since it was currently early September... Oh my God, it had almost been a year. No wonder I was so intrigued by the rando couple getting it on in a dark corner of a rooftop shindig.

The vicarious stimulation was too alluring. Softly, I tiptoed back around the silo, my body pressed against the edifice so I could just...peek.

Whoa. The sight was just as sultry the second time as it had been the first. More so now, when the woman's hips bucked up against his hand. It was downright filthy, the way he held her arms over her head, the way they didn't kiss, the only points of contact between them at her wrists and the place between her legs.

The next time she moaned, I almost moaned with her.

I made a note to self—*apparently you think voyeurism is hella hot.*

So hot that I'd forgotten all about why I'd come up here in the first place. So hot that my own pussy throbbed. So hot that I didn't think to slip back into hiding when she let out a final gasp and shuddered out her orgasm.

It was obviously when I should have left. Okay, I should have left earlier, but since I hadn't, this was the time. Yet, I stayed, entranced by the nonchalant attitude of her man as he pulled a hankie from inside his tux jacket and wiped off his hand before tucking it back into his pocket. Didn't even offer it to her.

It was evident the woman noticed. She scowled as she adjusted her dress, but her smile quickly returned. Throwing her brown tresses over her shoulder—dark but not as dark as mine—she sidled up to him, her hand lowering toward his crotch.

"Come on, Eden. You're finished." While I couldn't make out everything from my vantage point, I could clearly see him move her hand off of him.

"But you're not," she purred.

He stared at her for several seconds. I wished he was facing me so I could see his expression. It was so hard to spy on people who weren't cooperative.

"I'm not interested," he said finally. A dismissal, clear as day. I could tell that without having to see his face. "Only reason I got you off was so that you'd leave me alone."

Ouch.

This guy was a real asshole.

Or was he? He had given her what seemed to be an extremely proficient orgasm before blowing her off. Of course, I couldn't know enough to make the judgment from what I'd seen. But it was hard not to imagine details of the scenario as I stood by figuratively eating popcorn, and in my imagination, the guy was both fantastic at the sex and at the assholing.

The traits seemed to come in pairs from my experience.

Eden harrumphed, but she seemed to know when she was defeated. "Your loss. You know I treat you good."

"Yes, I do know. That's the problem."

Oh, yes, definitely a prick. The kind of guy who needed strange. The kind of guy who only messed with a girl once and moved on. Considering that the entire bar had been rented for an elite event, the one roaring on below us, I had this guy totally pegged. Rich. Entitled. Playboy. Eden would do best to walk away.

Her smile fell away, and she straightened her spine, her eyes throwing daggers. "You're an asshole."

My word exactly, Eden.

Playboy shrugged. "I warned you."

"You warned me knowing that by doing so you would come off as exactly the opposite. You know what? You deserve your misery."

She looked about to leave, which was my cue to skedaddle, but I hesitated when he reached out and grabbed her arm. "Eden, wait."

Her face softened with relief. Like she'd been hoping he'd stop her. I knew that hope. I was pretty sure Eden knew what she was in for when she'd gotten involved with this bastard, but still. It was hard not to empathize.

He let go of her arm and reached out to touch her face. Just when I thought playboy might not be so bad after all, he said, "Clean up before you go down there. Your mascara is smudged."

Eden jerked away, and with no further words, she stormed off.

Stormed *toward* me, actually.

Fuck.

I scurried around the silo, far enough around that she wouldn't see me as she descended the stairs, but not so far that the asshole would see me on the other side. Then I waited, listening for his footsteps so I'd know when it was safe to come out of hiding.

The asshole had a real quiet step, apparently, because I didn't hear squat. So I counted. To two hundred to be sure enough time had passed. It was a long two hundred, too, because I lost count a couple of times when an image of the sexy scene I'd walked into jumped into my head.

I was definitely adding *get laid* to my to-do list. This was ridiculous.

Finally, I poked my head around the silo to where I'd last seen him standing.

No one was there. I took a few more steps to be sure. He was nowhere in front of me. I sighed with relief.

"Looking for someone?"

I jumped at the voice behind me. Whirling around, I saw him standing in the shadows where I'd been just a few seconds before.

There was no way he'd known I was there. He couldn't have. He definitely couldn't have known I'd watched him. Quickly coming to that conclusion, I played innocent. "I thought I heard an animal. A cat in trouble. I was just looking around."

Awesome, Tess. That didn't sound super defensive at all.

"A cat. On a rooftop this high." He was rightly incredulous.

"It was odd to me too. Hence, why I was looking."

"Huh."

I was sweating with nervousness. I hadn't forgotten that I was at this event under false pretenses, and though there was no reason for this guy to question that right now, the fact put me on guard.

And not necessarily on guard in a good way. Because I should have stuck to my story—it was a true story, after all—and been on my way. He was still lingering in the shadows, his face cloaked in the dark. It wasn't like he was trying to stop me.

But there was a challenge behind that single syllable, an unspoken dare, and anyone who knew me knew I wasn't the type to walk away when the gauntlet was thrown.

I took a step toward him. "Huh? What's that supposed to mean? You don't believe me?"

He shrugged, the same couldn't-care-less shrug he'd given Eden. "I just meant huh."

"Oh." Maybe I'd imagined the dare. This whole ad-venture was a mistake. Why did I think I could pull this off without freaking out? I might be the kind of person who stood up to a challenge, but I wasn't an idiot, and coming to this party tonight had been crazy idiotic. And now I was making up drama where there wasn't any. "Okay, then," I said, turning away from the mystery man.

The same way he'd reached out with his hand to stop Eden, he reached out with his voice to stop me. "See, I think you did come looking because you heard something. Then you found something else. And instead of walking away...you stayed."

I pivoted back toward him. "I didn't—" I cut off abruptly. He'd stepped out of the shadows, and now, for the first time, I saw his face.

And it was stunning.

Take-your-breath-away stunning.

Panty-melting stunning.

No wonder Eden had been gaga over him. Everyday men didn't look like that. He was cover-model material. Pressed to describe him in words, I wouldn't have been able to explain what about him was so attractive. It was the whole package. The way his features knit together. His high cheekbones. The chiseled jaw evident under a well-trimmed beard, some shade of brown. His inset eyes—it was too dark to grasp their color, but the placement was perfection. And while it hid a lot from the backside, the tailored tux he wore showed enough from the front to see that he was very well-defined. Like, the kind of defined that not only owns a home gym but also spends time in it.

I'd been so surprised by him, so unprepared, that the words stumbled out before I had a chance to rein them in. "Oh, wow, you're hot."

Heat rushed up my neck into my face. My olive skin didn't show blush too easily, but the blood still ran upward when I embarrassed myself. And this was super embarrassing. Too embarrassing to even figure out how to fix.

While I was kicking myself and dying of shame, he swept in, smooth as a cucumber. "I was thinking the same thing about you."

And now he was hitting on me.
After he'd just gotten off another woman. I'd pegged him accurately, that was for sure. Player with a capital P.

I laughed, half nerves, half incredulity. "That's not. No. We're not. Uh-uh. Thanks, I'll just be leaving now."

I was too flustered to get all the way turned around this time before he halted me once again. "No, wait. I apologize. I didn't mean to come on strong. You said it first, so I took that as an invitation."

I considered for a beat before I responded—something I knew I should do more often. Okay, right. I had decided he was a playboy, but I didn't necessarily have proof. I had been the one who'd verbally vomited on a total stranger. I was definitely the one out of line.

"I did do that," I admitted. "I'm sorry. It just came out."

"No need to be sorry." His smile was like gold the way it gleamed. Hypnotic. He could convince a lot of women to do a lot of stupid things by flashing that beauty.

I hoped "a lot of women" didn't include me. But I was also realistic, so I was on high alert that it probably did.

And yet I was still standing there.

"Add that to the fact that you did stay through what you found up here." He was determined to make me admit to what I'd seen. It was a guess. He was feeling me out.

Really, though, was there a reason to deny it? I was more curious where he was taking this conversation, so I merely said, "And?"

"And that, combined with your comment on my appearance, gave me a different impression of where this interaction might be going." He prowled toward me. Literally. *Prowled.*

It was ridiculous how sexy a man could look just taking a handful of steps.

Even more ridiculous was how affected I was by it.

And, oh my God, it had taken me a beat, but had he really just said that?

"Please," I said, groaning in irritation that was meant for me as much as it was for him. "Because I accidentally walked in on your little sexcapade, you think that means I must want a sexcapade of my own?"

"No, of course not." That nonchalant shrug again. "It's the fact that you watched."

Another rush of blood to my cheeks. His back had been to me the entire time. Eden hadn't even seen me, and she'd been the one facing me. Was I wrong? Was there something reflective I'd missed on that brick wall? I swiveled to study where he'd been standing. I looked back to where I'd been standing.

Nope. No way. He hadn't seen me. I turned back to him with a gloating smile. "You couldn't know that."

Then it was his turn to gloat, because of course I'd just given away that I had, in fact, watched. "I was determining consent," I said on impulse.

"Looking out for your fellow woman."

"Exactly." I felt noble about the lie. As though I'd really been a hero instead of a peeping Tom, only concerned with whether or not Eden was being raped.

His smirk called bullshit, but he played along. "I hope you came to the conclusion that there was indeed consent."

"On her part anyway." I might have thought it was a dig when I first said it, but after the fact, even I knew it sounded like I was flirting.

Fuck. Maybe I was.

His expression seemed equally unsure. "I wasn't forced into anything. But yes, you're right. She didn't have my full attention. You, on the other hand, do." Unsure or not, he was awfully brave.

I had a thing for stupid-hot brave players.

And fooling around with one was definitely not on the night's agenda. I had to step away. "Okay, that's fine," I said, my head all jumbled and dazed. "Yep. I'm just. Thanks but no thanks. I just came up here to make a call and yeah. I'm going to go do that now." I had the sense to leave then. Even more sense to call over my shoulder, "Please don't follow me."

All right, maybe it wasn't sense that had me taking that last peek in his direction. I wanted to know if he was watching me walk away.

Call me an idiot because I was pleased to find he was.

TWO

Teyana answered on the first ring. "Tell me everything."

My head was still caught back in the silos with the irritating and irritatingly hot stranger. I probably should have waited for my temperature to cool before making my call, but I'd been eager to get on the phone so I'd look like I was doing something if he did happen to follow after me.

But he hadn't followed, and now I was stuck having to try to word.

I let out a sigh-groan. "Everything would be better if you were here," I said, which was the truth, but not something I would have said with such whine if I'd had my senses about me. Immediately, I tried to smooth it over. "I mean, I know it wouldn't be better for *you*, but it would be better for *me*, and I'm not trying to make you feel bad, I just like being with my friend."

Ugh, I was shitty. Worrying about my feelings and how sucky it was to have to be without her instead of focusing on the fact that she was actually physically suffering. I usually had a better grasp on the ways to be a good friend to someone with a chronic debilitating condition, but every now and then I failed big time.

"I'm sorry," I added, wishing I'd said that first.

"Hey, don't do that." As she was often wont to do, Tey slipped into the role of comforter. "I am well aware that my flare-ups are not just inconvenient for me."

"But that's the thing—they are *only* inconvenient for me. For you, they're so much more."

"Yeah," she agreed. "They're craptastic. I really do wish I was there with you instead."

That had been the original plan, for both of us to come together. Actually, when I'd seen the invite in my boss's mail, my plan had been to toss it in the trash and think no more about it, but Tey had grabbed it from my hands, her eyes bright with an idea.

"The invitation is for Kendra," I'd pointed out.

"They aren't going to ID people at the door. It says to bring the card for entry. This is all we need to get in."

"I wouldn't have anything to wear."

"You're house-sitting for a woman who has the largest selection of clothes outside Fifth Avenue. I bet some of her gowns still have the tags on them."

I'd considered it then. Kendra had loaned me and Teyana clothes a million times before, ever since the three of us met and became friends when we were pursuing our master's at Georgetown. Though we weren't quite as close as we'd been then—becoming her employee after gradu-ation had changed the dynamics of our relationship—she would likely still have let me borrow something if she'd been in town.

Of course, if she'd been in town, I wouldn't have been perusing her mail and wouldn't have known about the party in the first place.

Tey must have realized my acquiescence was flickering. *"Come on, Tess. When in our lives are we going to get to go to a party hosted by the Sebastians?"*

The Sebastians were American royalty. With their money divested in everything from steel and oil to media and tech, they practically owned the city. Their name was on as many buildings as the Rockefellers, including the Sebastian Center, the headquarters for most of their businesses in New York.

A party hosted by the fabulously rich was definitely tempting.

"Kendra wouldn't take us if she was here," Tey pressed on. *"This is once in a lifetime!"*

And because she'd been right about that, and because I'd been feeling more than a little bitter toward Kendra as of late, I said yes.

But then Teyana had a flare-up that had sent her to bed in the fetal position. I'd only agreed to still come so she could live vicariously through me. I'd been friends with her long enough to learn that sometimes the only thing I could do for her illness was live my own life to its fullest. In a lot of ways, Teyana being sick had pushed me further than I would have gone on my own.

That fact only made me feel guiltier.

"How are you feeling?" I asked now.

"Dizzy, and it feels like someone is repeatedly stabbing a long serrated knife between my ribs, but mostly I'm bored. Please unbore me and tell me about the party."

"Well." Honestly, I'd barely been at the party at all. I'd strolled from one side of the rooftop to the other, snagged a few exotic appetizers from trays as they passed by, and then snuck up the roped-off staircase to try to call her.

But that rendition of my evening wasn't going to unbore her, so I tried to fluff it up. "Everyone's dressed up, of course. Everything designer. I actually feel dressed down, and I'm wearing Dolce and Gabbana."

"I saw the pic you sent. You fit in, trust me."

I looked down at the pink skirt of tulle. "I look like a ballerina."

"You look prima and hot as fuck. End of subject. What else?"

"The music is club style. I thought it was going to be all classics and Frank Sinatra, but they have a mean beat going. I saw a couple of gray-hairs cutting it up on the dance floor, and I was actually impressed."

"I'm snoring here, Tess. Were you cutting it up on the dance floor with them? That's what I want to hear."

Of course I hadn't been dancing. That was Teyana's scene. I could have fun too, but I was more often the girl with her hand raised at the front of the classroom. It was why we worked so well as friends, and why I liked parties better with her at my side. It really wasn't fair that she was the one of us who was sick when she was so outgoing, and I was so not.

I wasn't going to go down the guilt-trip road again, though. What else could I tell her? The sex scene I'd witnessed, but I wasn't going to give her the good stuff first thing. "I didn't dance, but I ate! The food's really good, too. And weird. I couldn't name half of what I've put in my mouth."

"I'd appreciate that last sentence more if you weren't talking about food," she teased.

Okay, maybe it was time to bring out the filth. "Oh, I did watch a woman get finger-banged by a hot player in a fitted tux."

I could practically hear Teyana sit up with excitement. "Hallelujah, that's what I'm talking about. Please, please, please tell me there's more to this story. I need every single detail."

I laughed. "There isn't a lot to tell, unfortunately. I was looking for a quiet place to call you and came across them. Then, when I probably should have left them to it, I stayed for some reason."

"So you could tell me, obviously."

"Obviously. But when she was done, he dismissed her like she was nothing. And then—get this, Tey. Then, he had the nerve to hit on me." I was still blown away by his gall. And a bit flattered, which was fucked up because he probably hit on women all the time. Probably he'd already forgotten me.

"So you're meeting up with him after you hang up with me, right?"

"Uh, hardly."

She made an exasperated sound that was so heavy I felt it halfway across the city.

I couldn't believe her. "You want me to go hook up

with some sleazy rando who got it on with another woman already tonight?"

"It doesn't have to be *him*," she said. "But someone. For God's sake, you haven't been with anyone since Alejandro—"

I cut her off. "Not true. There was that guy at the Halloween party last year. Bob. Or Bobby. Whatever his name was."

"Which was almost a year ago, please, baby. You need to get laid. For me. Do it. Go find a mega-rich asswipe, and don't call me again until you're the one who's getting finger-banged."

It wasn't that easy for me. I knew sex was just sex, but I was a feely type of girl, which made for lots of tears considering the guys I seemed to fall for. It would be better if I was more like Tey. She could jump into bed with a guy she just met and never think about him again, no problem. In order to protect myself, I'd learned to hold out for the more romantic approach which meant at least three dates, and he damn well better call me after.

On the other hand, I'd had a couple of one-nighters that had ended just fine. When I'd gone in knowing what it was going to be, like with Bobby, I was able to walk away with no expectations and my heart intact. And it had been fun, too.

So maybe Tey was right. Six straight months of Match.com had led to nothing but a string of dates I'd rather leave forgotten. I had such a bad taste, romance wasn't even on my radar at the moment. Letting loose for one night might be a good way to reset.

With promises to do just that, I hung up. One thing was certain—if I was going to have the kind of fun Teyana hoped I'd have, I was going to need to hit the bar.

An hour and a half later, I was feeling the effects of three Mai Tais and the two shots that had preceded them. Conversation had definitely gotten easier. Though I'd sat myself at the main bar, I'd had several engaging interactions.

Currently, I was hitting on a hottie with green eyes and a wicked dimple. Or he was hitting on me. Whichever, it was promising.

"There she is again," Green Eyes said, ducking his head. "I swear she's not going to stop until she finds me."

I casually looked in the direction he'd nodded toward. He'd told me he was hiding from a woman when he'd first sat down next to me, but I hadn't quite decided if that was the truth or a line. I scanned for a woman who appeared to be looking for someone. "The blonde?"

He peeked up. "The woman next to her."

"Oh. The one old enough to be your grandma." I frowned. "Is she trying to get into your pants?" Green Eyes looked to be about my age, which was closer to thirty than I would have liked, even though it was still three years away.

"No, no, no." He paused as if imagining it. "God, no. Not anything against Adrienne Thorne, just…"

"It is rather a large age difference."

"More than thirty years, I think."

I laughed. "So if she's not after your manhood, why are you hiding?"

"It's stupid, really," he said with a blush. It was adorable how he could be so male and also vulnerable. He might not have the same effect on me that the asshole playboy had earlier, but if Green Eyes invited me home, I wouldn't be mad about it.

He wouldn't have to know I was thinking about someone else.

"I know stupid," I assured him. "Your stupidity is welcome here."

He smiled, letting his dimple fully shine. "I appreciate that, thank you. Adrienne is after me because she heard my company's looking to back a nonprofit. PR and philanthropy and all that. We've put it in our budget but haven't yet found the organization we want to sponsor. Anyway, she believes her charity would be the quote unquote perfect fit. It's not. I'd prefer to let her down in an office setting rather than ruin her evening."

My ears perked as though I were Pavlov's dog and a bell had rung. "Now would probably be a bad time to tell you that I match businesses with nonprofit sponsorships."

Well, *I* didn't. Kendra did. She built the company herself—her idea, her vision, her family's money as the seed. Me, I was more or less a glorified assistant, not what I'd set out to achieve when I'd accepted my scholarship to Georgetown, but it was a good paycheck, I didn't have to move back home, and in this day and age, wasn't that all a person could hope for?

Point was, I was involved enough in the ins and outs of the business that I knew how to sell it, and even though I'd been turned down by Kendra on several occasions when I'd asked to let me do just that, I was confident that I could do the job.

The dimple disappeared from Green Eyes' face.

"I'm sorry," I said, realizing my faux pas. "Here you are trying to enjoy your night, and I'm turning it into business."

"That's not what I was thinking at all. I'm actually interested. Like I said, we're after a sponsorship. In fact, we're behind our deadline at selecting one. I just thought maybe it was too presumptuous of *me* to try to pursue that at a party."

Oh, I liked this guy. Willing to turn pleasure into business at the drop of a good opportunity—that was my kind of man.

On the other hand—I looked down at my empty glass—I had consumed quite a bit of alcohol. And Teyana would kill me if I walked out of this with a deal rather than a fuck.

Besides, I couldn't do shit without Kendra and not only was she out of town for who knew how long "finding herself," but there was also no way I was admitting to her that I'd stolen her invite.

"Tell you what," Green Eyes said, apparently sensing my hesitation. "I don't have a business card on me. Give me your phone."

Without questioning him, I unlocked my cell and handed it to him.

He tapped away on my device. "I'm adding Julie Sanchez to your contacts. That's my assistant. Call her next week and schedule an appointment. What was the name of your organization? I'll give her a heads-up."

It wasn't enough time for me to think up a lie, so I told the truth. "Conscience Connect." Maybe I could pass the info on to Kendra without telling her how I got it. It was part of my job to find leads for her after all.

"Fantastic. I look forward to discussing more." He gave me back my phone, his eyes focused somewhere behind me. "Meanwhile, I've been spotted. I have to get out of here. Hopefully we'll see each other again later."

His last words were full of all the heat I'd been looking for earlier in the conversation. Too bad there wouldn't be a later. Now that I'd given him Conscience Connect, a hook-up was out of the question. It would be too easy for him to figure out who I was—or rather who I wasn't—and friend or not, I wasn't about to risk my position with Kendra.

But maybe if I hooked up her company with his...

"Wait," I said, realizing I'd neglected to get some crucial information. I skimmed the crowd. "I don't even know your name." I was talking to myself, though, because he'd disappeared.

"I'm pretty sure you can just refer to him as Mr. Sebastian when you call his secretary," the bartender said. "Can I get you a refill?"

I ignored the question and the fact that he'd been eavesdropping because I was currently freaking out. "He was a Sebastian?" My face felt hot and it had nothing to do with the alcohol I'd been drinking. I'd been talking to a celebrity. A Sebastian in the flesh. Thank goodness I hadn't known before. I would have definitely said something stupid.

It was possible I'd said something stupid anyway. I scanned back through our conversation looking for anything cringeworthy. Everything I could recall was pretty banal.

This definitely meant I couldn't pass the info on to Kendra, though. I'd already tried to suggest approaching the Sebastians on several occasions, and she'd instantly nixed it every time. Something about their family being too close to hers, wasn't appropriate, blah blah blah. I wasn't a rich girl. I didn't understand all the rules of society.

Too bad because Mr. Sebastian and I had had a connection. I was pretty sure I could have sold him. What a deal that would have been.

"Oh my God, he was a Sebastian," I repeated to myself.

"There are several of them around here," a voice said at my side. An annoyingly delicious and familiar voice. "Dime a dozen."

I turned to find myself face-to-face with the stupid-hot player, and damn if he wasn't even hotter close-up. "You," I said, a bit scornfully because I was feeling contemptuous about the way he lit every nerve in my body on fire.

"You," he said in turn. His tone seemed to both appreciate my scorn and know full well the source of it. "I was hoping we'd meet again."

"I was hoping we wouldn't."

"Funny, I don't believe you."

He wasn't an idiot, and the truth was glaringly evident. I couldn't stop staring. My eyes were magnetically drawn to him. He was so gorgeous, it made me need to take a seat, and I was already sitting. His hair was lighter, I realized, than I'd figured in the dark. Brownish-red with golden hues, so perfectly messy in distribution that it had to be natural. His eyes were a killer blue. I'd always been a sucker for blue eyes. And for stupid-hot player types. It was like he'd been ordered up for me specifically, a Tessa Turani cocktail guaranteed to make me mind-numbingly drunk from just looking at him.

"Can I buy you a shot?" he asked, as if I needed alcohol when he was in my system.

Somehow I managed to pull my gaze away. "It's an open bar."

"In that case, I can afford to buy you two." He summoned the bartender who hadn't gone far, that nosy little spy. "Four shots of…" Blue Eyes looked at me. "Tequila all right?"

How had he known? "The source of many a bad decision."

"Tequila it is."

He was so smooth. Much smoother than the liquor would be, I knew from experience.

Yet, I didn't object when the bartender put the four shots in front of us, along with a shaker of salt and a bowl of limes.

Just seeing the setup made me want to take my clothes off. Or maybe it was Blue Eyes that did that. He knew how to fill a tux, and I had a feeling he looked even better with it off.

He and the bartender knew exactly where this was going. How dumb was I?

I held up a single shot. "A little obvious, don't you think?"

"That I want to be one of your bad decisions?" He lifted one as well. "I thought honesty was deserved after what we've been through together."

"As if we've gone through a bonding experience."

"I found it incredibly bonding. See, you watched." He leaned in close, lowering his voice to a rasp that only I could hear. "And I find that very, very hot."

A shiver ran down my spine. Yeah, I needed the tequila. Skipping the salt, I shot the first glass back then reached for a lime. I cringed, not just from the sour taste but from the words he'd said and my reaction to them.

I shook my head. "And you're bonded with women that you find hot?"

"Temporarily," he grinned. "Yes."

That smile was a serious weapon. "There's that honesty again," I said, pretending that I wasn't doomed. "I should give you credit for it."

"You should." He poured back his own shot, no salt, no lime. He was letting me know he was hardcore, in case that did it for me.

Of course it did. My type to a T.

Perhaps it was because he was so perfectly my weakness that I continued to fight it. "Just because I watched didn't mean that I found it hot."

"But you did."

"I never said that." I'd said I found *him* hot. It wasn't the same thing.

He shrugged as if the semantics didn't matter. "You didn't have to."

No, I didn't. I was a puddle of wet for him. He didn't have to put his hand between my legs to know.

I swiveled toward him, finally giving in. I lifted the second drink up so that we could clink them together when he lifted his. We shot them back together, and though I tried to resist, I broke down and sucked on the lime.

I could feel his eyes on me as I did, scorching with their intensity. I could practically hear his thoughts. *She'll taste like citrus when I kiss her.*

I had to cross my legs to ease the ache. "Who said you were the reason I watched?" This time I was flirting. Teyana would be so proud when I told her later. "Maybe it was Eden I found hot."

"It wasn't."

He'd gotten closer, somehow without even seeming to move. Instead of two people sitting next to each other, we were two people sharing one space. His body pressed against the outside of my thigh. I could feel that touch everywhere. My nipples steepled like antennas attempting to draw more of that electricity in.

He reached out to brush a lock of my hair behind my ear, then let his fingers trail down my neck.

"You're rather sure of yourself," I whispered.

"Tell me your name. I'll make you sure of me too."

I stood up in a sudden panic. "No. No names."

"I didn't think it was possible, but I'm even more

turned on."

On my feet, the world felt a hell of a lot less steady. It was the alcohol, of course, but also it was him, this charming brute of a man. Saying charming things and smiling his charming smile and gazing at me with his charming blue eyes.

Dumb and doomed. That was me. "I think I should leave."

"Let me take you."

I knew I couldn't agree to that. Letting him take me to the apartment I shared with Teyana in Jersey City would be as bad as giving him my name. Besides, I was staying at Kendra's, and I definitely couldn't lead him there.

But I'd had enough drinks to make it difficult to think straight, and if he was offering to take me to *his* home, we both knew the answer wasn't no.

THREE

My trip to the lobby would have been embarrassing if I'd been sober enough to recognize it. Walking was impossible without holding on to Blue Eyes' arm, which I clutched onto for dear life. Truth be told, I would have clutched it anyway. It would have been a shame to ignore it once he'd offered it. Even with the material of his tux between my hand and his bicep, I could tell it was a very nicely shaped bicep.

I'm pretty sure I told him so in the elevator because Blue Eyes turned to the elderly couple who was riding with us. "She has a thing for toned biceps."

"I actually do," I said with a smile.

The returning smile from the couple wasn't quite as polite.

When we were out of the elevator, one glance at the distance to the outside doors, and I knew I wasn't going to make it, even with the help of toned biceps. "Hold on," I said. Pressing a palm to his chest for support, I bent over and worked off one of the sky-high sandals, then the other.

"Much better," I sighed when my bare feet met the marble floor.

"I'm pretty sure there's a no shoes, no entrance policy." But from his tone of voice and the glint in his eyes, I gathered he was more amused than concerned.

"Better get me outside then quick."

He didn't waste a single second ushering me out of the building. When we got to the curb, he only had to nod to the doorman, and his car pulled up, as if it had been waiting for him. Blue Eyes was smoother than I'd realized—I hadn't even seen him pull out his phone, and he must have called or texted ahead for such quick service.

I would have remarked on the fact if I hadn't been so distracted by the car itself. "A limo?"

"The Maybach's in the shop."

I assumed it was a joke, but it might not have been. Considering he'd actually been invited to the froufrou party upstairs, he might very well have owned a high-class Mercedes. More likely, he'd rented the limo and was simply trying to impress.

I *was* impressed. I was also stubborn enough not to let on. "I suppose it will do." I handed my shoes to Blue Eyes then slid across the back bench. "Comfy."

"Glad you approve." He was smirking when he joined me. And despite all the ample room in the vehicle, he sat pretty darn close.

I had to catch my breath. "Well, hello."

"Hello yourself."

This close, in the confines of such a small place, I could smell his rosewood cologne. Or maybe it was sandalwood.

I wasn't experienced enough with male fragrances to be able to correctly identify more than the fact that it was woody, and it smelled nice. And that it was the kind of scent that made me heady and outside myself.

That could also have been the copious amounts of liquor.

Whatever the cause, I knew then that I was in real trouble with this boy.

A well-mannered voice boomed through a speaker near my head. "Destination, sir?"

Blue Eyes reached past me to hit an intercom button, then he looked to me, as though waiting for me to say something.

Oh, fuck. He wanted my address.

It was appropriate, I supposed. Allowing me to direct where this would go next instead of making assumptions. Even drunk I recognized it as admirable.

I was a little annoyed at the same time. I resented having to be the one to make the decision and almost wished he would have just given the order to go to his place, and then I could have feigned shock and dismay while secretly being thrilled and relieved.

So it was my job to say the words. *Take me to your place.* It was on the tip of my tongue.

But I was headstrong and wanted a little more of the chase. "Could we just drive around awhile?"

"You heard the lady." His grin said he didn't mind more of the chase himself.

The car jolted into motion, the swerve out of the drive into traffic throwing me in his direction. He caught me in his arms, and my heartbeat stuttered. There was so much wild energy between us, I could barely handle being held by him like this. And we still had all our clothes on. *Doomed, I say.*

"Doomed?"

Shit. Hadn't meant to say that aloud.

Needing to take hold of my dignity, I pulled out of his arms. "Wasn't ready for the car to start. Aren't there seatbelts in these things?"

There *was* a seatbelt, it turned out, but as soon as I started examining the vehicle's interior, I found many other features to appreciate. "You have a printer? In your car?" I shut the cabinet that had revealed the computer and charging station and opened another to find a television. This was not like the party limo from my trip to Vegas. "What's on your side?"

"The fridge. The bar. Can I get you something to eat? Some water?" He was studying me like he wanted to devour me. It was his restraint that made me squirm the most.

I wondered how Eden had borne it as well as she had. She'd come away from their encounter with a bit of smudged makeup, but she was at least able to hold her head up. I wasn't sure I'd be able to leave this car at anything but a crawl.

The encounter with Eden back in my head had me suddenly wary. "Was she your girlfriend?"

"Who?"

It was amazing how patient he was with my subject jumps, as though he was ready to follow anywhere I led.

"Eden."

"Oh. No. No." He dragged the last no out like the idea was ludicrous.

I believed his answer, but I'd known manipulative men before. The kind who rely heavily on the questions worded. *You asked if she was my girlfriend, not if I was married.* "Your wife?"

"Nope." He guessed my next question before I asked. "No one else is either."

I had already checked out his hand and found neither a band nor a tan line. Even just a one-night encounter, I refused to be party to infidelity.

I pivoted so I was facing him. "So nobody has reason to later say you cheated by being in this car with me?"

His hand found its way to rest on my knee. Lightly, above my skirt. Nothing scandalous, and yet I felt thoroughly scandalized. "That kind of accusation would require something to happen between us. Right now, all I've done is offer a beautiful woman a ride home."

"I'm not going to be distracted by the charm, you charm...whore."

He laughed. "Charm-whore?"

"I know, it didn't even make sense in my head. And you avoided the question."

His eyes moved from mine to the hand on my knee that was now toying with the tulle, as though he were inspecting the fabric instead of casually planning his voyage underneath. "I am not currently obligated to anyone in any way."

"Okay." I relaxed a little. Let myself start to accept that I was really going to do this. I was really going to let this filthy-hot rich man have his filthy-hot way with me.

I never let my guard down easily, though, and I was curious by nature. "Then how did that hookup even transpire? You weren't into her, you weren't obliged to her... Why would you even...?"

"Do you really want to spend this time talking about Eden?"

I shivered as his palm met the bare flesh of my lower thigh even though the touch itself was searing. "I just..." What had I been saying? What had I been thinking? "I mean, if you're that nice to a girl you aren't interested in, how nice are you to a girl you like?"

"Lucky you, you're about to find out." He bent forward then, and I raised my face thinking he was coming in for my lips. Instead, he landed on my jaw, and whoa. Somehow that was even more electrifying, the press of his open mouth against my skin, an almost kiss. A tease. A taunt.

I turned my head to chase after him, but he'd already moved on, lower, to my neck. Without thinking to do so, I tilted my chin up, giving him better access. Of course, as soon as I gave him that, he'd advanced again, peppering kisses down my décolletage before kissing along my breasts where they swelled above the dress.

He was fast, giving me no time to adjust to one sensation before giving me another, and yet it also felt achingly slow. I arched my back, a silent plea for him to discover more of me, *all* of me. My nipples ached with a need so urgent, I half wished he would tear the bust of my dress down so he could get to them. I didn't even care that it wasn't *my* dress that I'd be sacrificing nor that I didn't have the five grand to pay Kendra back for its destruction.

Fortunately for my future self who very much wanted to keep her employment, Blue Eyes had other plans. Abruptly he shifted, and next thing I knew, he was on the ground in front of me. On his knees, his mouth in my lap, kissing first above my navel before moving to the apex of my thighs.

Even with the layers of tulle, I felt his mouth there, pressed against my clit, and if I hadn't been before, I certainly was wet now.

"You smell incredible," he said, his voice rough, like my scent had a potent effect on him.

Holy hell, he was dirty.

And I was there for it. I pressed my knees apart, making space for him.

"Is that an invitation? Because I can't go any further unless it is."

Oh, he was good. "Don't tell me you're the kind of guy who makes a woman ask for it."

His fingers circled around my ankles, and even so far away from where I wanted them, I felt the jolt on my pussy as though they were there instead. "You had been awfully concerned about consent earlier." He trailed the tips of his fingers up the side of my calves, to the outside of my knees.

"I was concerned when it was Eden. Personally, I prefer a little less give and a little more take."

That was all the permission he needed. With a firm yank, my ass was pulled to the edge of the bench, then my knees pushed together, which confused me until I realized his goal was the removal of my panties. I was at once grateful that I'd worn my prettiest white lace and also regretful when he stashed them in his jacket pocket, and I realized I'd never see them again.

Worth the price, I decided when my knees were pressed open again, my dress pushed up, and I saw the expression on his face.

Devastated. That's how he looked. Completely devastated, in all the good ways.

Now he knew how I felt.

Reverently, he stroked the tip of his finger down my seam. "This is a pretty pussy."

My skin felt hot everywhere. No one had ever said anything like that to me before. I couldn't decide if I was mortified or just really fucking turned on. I decided to lean into the latter. "Yeah?" I asked, wanting to hear it again.

"Oh, yeah."

I wanted him to say more, but then he leaned forward and traced his tongue along the same path his finger had made, and suddenly there was only one thing I wanted his mouth to be doing, and it wasn't talking.

"Taste as good as you smell," he said when he'd reached my opening.

"Don't stop, don't stop, don't stop." So much for not wanting to give. I was practically begging.

He chuckled but went back to task, the vibration and his beard rubbing my pussy in just the right way.

I let out a whimper as he parted my folds and zeroed the tip of his tongue in on the buzzing nerve bundle. Only a handful of licks in, and I was already seeing stars. Magic. He was magic, and I was unraveling faster than a spool of thread in the possession of a kitten. My thighs shook, my pussy clenched, my clit was on fire. Had oral sex always felt so good? It couldn't have. I would certainly have remembered it, would have encouraged Alejandro to perform it more often instead of only the four or five times he did during our two-year relationship. There was something else at work. The amount of alcohol I'd had, perhaps. Or the length of time since I'd last been laid.

"That's why," I said, deciding the latter was definitely the reason.

Magic man between my thighs lifted his mouth but replaced the pressure on my clit with his chin. "Why what?"

Oh, wow. The scratch of his beard against my sensitive skin was as mind-blowing as everything else he'd done. I stretched my hands above my head, giving into the pleasure. "Why it feels so good. Because it's been so long."

"So long since...what?"

I couldn't even mind that he was chatty, not when he was still doing magic. "Since I got laid."

"Has it been a while?"

"Too long. And so this feels super amazing."

And now his finger was helping out, circling around the rim of my opening, teasing it with entry. I bucked my hips, urging more. Urging him inside.

His mouth returned to my clit. This time instead of a stroke of his tongue, he sucked and damn, I was instantly close to coming. "That's why it feels good," he said with a not-so subtle hint of sarcasm. "No other reason."

Who was I fooling? Certainly not him, and even intoxicated I knew that I was only barely fooling myself.

That last little thread of self-deceit vanished with the next little trick of his mouth, some sort of lick, flick, and suck combination that took me to the edge.

The edge where he left me when he sat back on his knees. "Because it's been so long."

"Okay, okay, you're good!" I was desperate to get him back, to finish me off, and I would have said anything, including, apparently, the truth.

"Good?"

"Really, really good." The words were far from adequate, but he had mercy on me and picked up right where he'd left off, pushing me off the ledge into an epic spiral of a climax. I cried out at the release, my body seizing as the pleasure rippled over me, leaving me panting and boneless and euphoric all at once.

Blue Eyes, I learned then, was not only a magic man but a cruel one. Because he wasn't finished with me. His tongue and mouth worked with even more fervor, and his fingers were no longer shy, plowing into me two, three at a time with delicious assault.

There was no more talking, though. My ability to speak had been taken away. Everything that tumbled from my lips after that was nonsensical single syllables and pure sound.

And while thoughts of Eden were far from my mind as well as any desire to make this encounter more than what it was, what it had to be—a one-night stand—a fleeting curiosity swirled through the chaos of pleasure: if Blue Eyes finger-banged girls he didn't like and went down this spectacularly on those he did, just how well would he treat a girl he loved?

FOUR

I woke up to the sound of a jackhammer.

I sat up, startled, and immediately regretted it when my stomach lurched from the movement. Thank God the room was mostly dark. Even the small slit of light coming from behind the blackout curtains was enough to make my eyes hurt. My head, too. Though most of that pain seemed to be associated with the terrible hammering.

I rested back against the wall and closed my eyes, trying to calm the headache and get a sense of balance before figuring out how to deal with the world. I took a deep, cleansing breath. In. Out.

Wait a minute.

It was only a handful of seconds later when my eyes flew open again. Having spent the last several days at Kendra's, I'd gotten used to waking up somewhere other than my own bed. But not only was this not my bedroom, it also wasn't hers. And I hadn't the faintest recollection of arriving there.

I scanned the room for something to jog my memory.

I was alone. Nothing was familiar. Not the rustic wood floors nor the plush gray rug nor the tall modern lamp at the side of the bed nor the sleek black wall behind me. Definitely a male's room. Everything about it screamed man, including the vague musky scent. It wasn't until I'd spotted my dress—rather, Kendra's dress—draped over the back of an armchair I'd never seen before in my life, that I realized I was naked.

I clutched the sheet around me in what was likely a much-too-late attempt at modesty. What had happened last night? I remembered the party. The shots. Blue Eyes. The limousine.

Oh my God, the limo.

Three incredible orgasms—or was it four? After that, everything went blank.

I would have been less irritated at the fact that I'd obviously gone home with Blue Eyes if I had the pleasure of remembering it.

The jackhammering stopped suddenly, though the pain that accompanied it still vibrated in my head, and I was pretty sure it hadn't been an actual jackhammer but something more domestic. Coffee grinder?

Shit. He was making breakfast. The whiff of bacon in the air confirmed it. And though the idea of a man making breakfast was very appealing, there was no way I could stay for this. I'd taken too much of a risk even getting in the car with him. He could have found out that I hadn't actually been invited to that party, and if word got back to my boss... Not to mention that he was a stranger, and I hadn't told a soul where I was going.

Well, he'd said he wanted to be one of my mistakes. *Congratulations, Blue Eyes, you just may have landed the top spot.*

I had to get out of there. I didn't have any idea what the layout of the apartment was, but maybe I could slip out while he was distracted. After a quick trip to the en suite bathroom, I put my dress back on as quickly as I could without throwing up. My shoes and purse were next to the chair, as if they'd been laid out for me. My panties, I suspected, had been tucked away as a souvenir because they were nowhere in sight. My phone was almost dead, but I was able to shoot off a quick text to Teyana.

> Went home last night with the pervert from the roof. Tell you more later. If I disappear, here's where I was last.

I sent her a GPS ping giving her my location, then tucked my cell in my purse, grabbed my shoes, and tiptoed out of the room. A short hallway led to a living room. A formal dining room was next to that. Both were immaculate and spectacularly designed. I didn't have to be an art aficionado to guess that the multicolored modern painting on the wall cost a fortune. The floor-to-ceiling windows let in the perfect amount of light to show it off. One thing was for sure—Blue Eyes had cash. Which made sense. He'd actually been invited to the Sebastian party, and from what I'd learned from knowing Kendra, those rich folks tended to hang out in packs.

As much as I wanted to stay and explore, top of my agenda was sneaking out unseen. I had two options for my route of escape: another hallway or a swinging door that led to another room, likely the kitchen.

Hallway it is.

A couple of yards down this one, and another hall broke off to the right, this one leading to—hallelujah—the front door. I'd made it.

Except, halfway there, a figure stepped out from a door to the right, another entry to the kitchen, apparently. Blue Eyes had looked good in a tux. Wearing nothing but gray sweatpants, he was absolutely sinful. Rock-solid abs highlighted his bare chest. A perfectly toned arm held a black coffee mug, which he held inches below his devilish smirk.

"Sneaking out?"

"Uh…" I smiled guiltily.

He took a casual sip from his mug, appearing to not be at all bothered by my intentions to leave without a goodbye. "I made eggs and bacon if you'd like a bite to eat before you go. Fresh orange juice and ground coffee too."

It was tempting. Even though the sound of food made my stomach churn, the image of him cooking for me, serving me, got my pulse racing.

Honestly, he just got my pulse racing in general. The chemistry between us was wickedly charged. Whatever had happened between us last night, it hadn't been enough to run the heated energy to its end. A fleeting image of what might transpire if I stayed flashed through my mind—me bent over his kitchen table, his body pressed to mine as he entered me from behind.

Nope, nope, nope. "Sorry. I'm running late," I lied.

"On a Sunday?"

"Church." My face went warm. Did I really suggest I was going to church? Once it was out, there was nothing to do but run with it. "Really devoted to my congregation. Never miss a week. I'm going to have to go home and change first, though. So…"

His lips twitched with amusement, and I wondered for half a second if he was going to call me out on the fabrication. Then he said, "I'll have my driver take you."

"Already called an Uber." I dug out my phone from my purse and waved it in the air. I hoped I had enough battery to actually call for one when I got downstairs.

"Cancel it."

How did he manage to be both commanding and pleading at once? My chest fluttered in response. Why did I have to have met him the way I did? If my deceit wasn't tangled up with our meeting…

But there never would have been an occasion for me to meet a man like him at all without my deceit. That's how it was for girls from my side of the tracks. We had to hustle just to get the scraps.

My hesitation or my expression must have told him all he needed to know. "Okay. No ride. You don't want me to know where you live. I can take the hint."

Good.

Why did it feel so bad? And not the good kind of bad. The kind of bad that I was sure Blue Eyes was really good at being.

"Well, then." I forced myself to cross to his door. When he was behind me, I paused to slip one shoe on, then the other.

He didn't move. I could feel him watching me, the heat of his gaze searing into my backside. "At least tell me your name," he said after several seconds had passed.

"No reason to know it now." My hand was on the knob.

"I don't accept that. Without your name, how am I supposed to see you again?"

Bingo.

But I didn't want to be that blunt. It wasn't his fault I had to cut this off right now. In other circumstances, I would have been all over his invitation for breakfast. I would have been all over him period. Knowing it was an impossible fantasy, I threw my head over my shoulder and gave him one last flirty smile. "I don't know, Blue Eyes. Maybe you'll find me anyway. You seem like that kind of guy."

I had the door open before he took his first step toward me. "Blue Eyes? Is that how you're going to refer to me when you think of me in the future?"

I paused before turning toward him. I wanted to ask him why he was so sure that I'd think of him, but I didn't have the energy to deny what we both knew was the truth. "It's your most notable feature," I said instead.

I let the door go, but it didn't shut in time to block off his last words. "In that case, I'll remember you as Pretty Pussy."

I walked on shaky knees to the elevator. If I'd had any sense at all, I would have run.

FIVE

"I'm dying. Literally dying." Teyana leaned on our kitchen island, the tomato and salt sandwich she'd been making abandoned as she'd become engrossed in my story of the previous evening, particularly the parts about my mysterious one-night stand.

"Considering how often you say that, I think you might not have a good grasp on the meaning of the word *dying* and/or the word *literally*." Often when she used the term, she was curled up in the fetal position with pain. Today she was bouncing with excitement. I was happy to see she was feeling better.

She rolled her so-dark-brown-they-were-almost-black eyes at me. "You know what I mean. I can't believe you had such an incredible night. Good for you. You needed it."

I resisted the urge to feel bad that I'd been having my incredible night while she'd been miserable and focused on enjoying the retelling for her sake. "You're right. I did need it." I reached over the island to grab a tomato off her plate. I'd already been to Kendra's to drop off the dress and change before coming out to Jersey City, and I was only now getting an appetite. "Too bad I got so drunk. Best sex of my life, and I don't even remember it."

"How do you know it was the best sex of your life then?"

"Based on what I do remember, there's no way it wasn't. He knew exactly what he was doing. Three times." Just remembering made my panties damp. *Pretty Pussy,* he'd said. I really should have named him Filthy Mouth instead of Blue Eyes.

Tey sighed dreamily. "I don't think I could come three times with my vibrator. This man must be a god."

"Or a devil. Is it possible to be both?"

"I think you've just described every man you've ever dated more than two weeks." She smacked my hand as I reached for another tomato slice. "There's too much salt on that for a healthy person, Tess. Cut up your own if you want some."

Feigning a pout, I reached for a banana in the fruit basket instead. "He really was exactly my type. Which means it's probably a good thing that I'm not seeing him again since my type always leads to disaster."

Tey brought her sandwich up to her mouth and paused before biting into it. "Disaster is not inevitable with the guys you like. It's just how it's worked out."

"Yeah, yeah." I didn't want this to lead to another one of her lectures about being patient, there were loads of fish in the sea. It was hard to hear it over and over, and not to be snide, but it wasn't like she had a steady man of her own at the moment.

I also didn't think it was a good idea to keep talking about Blue Eyes. Thinking about him did a number on my libido. I was already looking forward to alone time later tonight when I was back in Kendra's guest room. For now, I needed to think about something else.

Maybe a banana hadn't been the best choice.

I shook the thoughts about the phallic shape of the fruit in my hand and took a bite. "Oh, I almost forgot to tell you. I met a Sebastian."

"You what?" She had to set down her sandwich. "Are you freaking serious?"

"Yep."

"Which one?"

"No idea." I quickly told her about my encounter with Green Eyes, including how he'd programmed his assistant's info in my phone.

"Give it here." Teyana reached her hand out for my cell.

I hesitated for a minute wondering what she was up to, but curiosity won out, and I unlocked the screen before giving it over. "What are you going to do?"

"This." She dialed the number and put it on speaker so we could both hear.

"There won't be anyone there on Sunday," I said as the phone rang.

"I know, but there will be a voicemail." Sure enough, the ringing switched over to a prerecorded message that announced we'd reached Julie Sanchez at the office of public relations for Sebastian Industrial Corporation.

"That wasn't helpful."

But she wasn't done. She quickly clicked END on the call then pulled up my internet browser. Less than a minute later, she had the SIC website's leadership page loaded. She scrolled through several positions filled by various Sebastians—Blue Eyes was right; there were a ton of them—until she landed on the name next to Vice President of Image and Outreach. "Scott Sebastian," she read. "That has to be the head of PR. Dammit, there's no image. Was he cute?"

"Scott Sebastian," I repeated, trying to picture the man who'd wanted to talk shop. "I guess he looked like he could be a Scott. And yes, he was fine with a capital F. He was really flirty. If he hadn't been hiding, I think I could have gone home with him."

"Oh my God, you settled!"

I shook my head, laughing. "I wouldn't have traded Blue Eyes for the hottest Sebastian in the world. Besides. It was risky enough going home with just another attendee at the party. If I'd gone home with a Sebastian and then he'd found out that I'd snuck my way in—"

"He wouldn't have found out, and if he did, do you think he'd really care?"

Yeah, she was right. I was being paranoid. "Better to be safe than sorry." But now I was thinking about the other opportunity I'd been denied because of caution. "Why did I have to meet him like that, Tey? He's looking for a charity for Sebastian Industrial to back. I could have pitched to them."

"You still could. You have his number. Set up a meeting."

"And then what? Even if they decided to go with one of the charities I presented, I wouldn't be able to go anywhere after the initial pitch without Kendra."

She thought about it for too long, the expression on her face saying she was taking this way too seriously.

"Whatever you're thinking, Tey—"

She interrupted me. "If you pitched them the Dysautonomia Foundation, you could do it without Kendra. Didn't Sarah offer you a job there? You could quit working for Kendra and work for them directly instead of being the liaison."

"Okay, no. No." There were so many immediate problems, I couldn't let myself entertain the idea. "First, they'd have to choose the Dysautonomia Foundation from the portfolio of charities I offered. If they chose any other, I'd be screwed."

"You could make them pick it. Your enthusiasm would sell it alone."

I ignored her. "Second, I wouldn't even know how to do a pitch meeting. I've only been on the backend."

"You could wing it. I saw you ace several projects in school that I know you put together on the fly."

"Third, I don't want to quit working for Kendra."

"Don't you?"

Here, I hesitated. The thing was, I *could* wing it. And I did have a passion for promoting the Dysautonomia Relief Foundation. I'd been trying to get Kendra to hook them up with a major sponsor for over two years now, pretty much as soon as Teyana got her dysautonomia diagnosis. But it wasn't just because of Tey that I supported the foundation. It was a good organization with lots of promise. I was convinced the only reason it hadn't been picked up yet was because Kendra wasn't selling it right. If I were the one presenting it, I knew I could sell it.

And one day Kendra would let me pitch it. She would. I had to believe that. Otherwise, all the years I'd stuck by her side were just a waste of time. "If I wanted to leave her, I would have taken the job Sarah offered."

"You're too loyal," Tey said with a sigh. "Kendra does not deserve that kind of loyalty."

"Maybe not." But I was loyal to Teyana too, and I couldn't risk the foundation's chances of being chosen by doing this underhandedly.

I expected the discussion to be over. It's certainly where it should have ended.

But Teyana didn't give up that easily. "Then you'd stay with Conscience Connect. That works too. Land the Sebastians, and there's no way Kendra can let you go. Plus, she'd get to see what you can do, and she'd have to give you more responsibility. Win-win all around."

"I don't know…" I could already imagine a plethora of things that could go wrong. I'd seen Kendra work on deals that signed instantly. Others required weeks and weeks of hardcore negotiation. I'd learned enough from the sidelines that I was fairly sure I could seal up the former with no problems. I wouldn't know the first thing about how to handle the latter.

Maybe if I knew I had enough time to work it out...

Tey read my mind. "How long is Kendra out of town?"

"Your guess is as good as mine."

"She was gone, what? Two months when she broke up with that guy three years ago."

"But only two weeks when she broke up with that girl she was dating last year."

I watched her fingers tap on the counter. She wore fingerless gloves, even though the air conditioning wasn't on and it was well in the nineties outside. Her particular syndrome made it hard for her body to regulate temperature, and often her extremities were blue and icy regardless of the weather. Other symptoms that accompanied her illness prevented her from working a full-time job, yet she wasn't bad enough to file for disability. Without help from the Dysautonomia Relief Foundation, she wouldn't be able to afford to live.

How many other women could be helped by the DRF if they had corporate sponsorship? Could I really try to fight for it?

"This latest disappearance wasn't even due to a breakup," I said, wondering if Kendra was distraught enough to keep her away for long. "She said she's torn between two lovers and needs time for her heart to decide."

"Yeah, that sounds like her prosey bullshit." Her tone was spiteful. She'd apologize eventually. That was how it usually went, anyway.

I chewed on my lip, giving her a few minutes to eat her sandwich and brood in silence.

I understood why Teyana was so bitter toward Kendra, but it still made me sad. Once upon a time we'd all been friends, when we were in school and our social statuses were on a more even playing field. That was before Tey got sick. Before we realized just exactly how well-off the Montgomery family was. It wasn't until after graduation that we discovered that our education, though exactly the same on paper, wasn't equal in the real world. Kendra Montgomery had doors opened for her at every turn. Tey and I had to fight from the ground up, and six years later, we hadn't gotten very high up the ladder. And it wasn't about the color of our skin since I was the whitest of the three of us.

At first Kendra seemed to care. She'd given me a job. She'd donated money to the DRF in Tey's name so she would be guaranteed funds. But she also stopped hanging out with Teyana all together. Seemed a friend with an ailment was too much work for her. She preferred to write a check and walk away.

I'd been stuck in the middle. I appreciated that it was Kendra who made it possible for Tey not to have to work full-time, but I hated how she'd broken Tey's heart and destroyed her self-confidence. I couldn't admit out loud that I still hoped they'd patch things up one day. It was another reason why I wasn't ready to leave Conscience Connect. I was still holding out for the dream ending all around.

My phone rang on the kitchen island where Tey had left it. She was closer so she glanced at it first. "Speak of the devil." With a scowl, she pushed the phone toward me.

I looked at the screen for confirmation. RESTRICTED, it said. The only person who called me from restricted lines was Kendra. I let out a sigh then, knowing she'd hear it in my voice if I didn't, I put on a bright smile and answered. "K! How's the vacation?"

"It's not a vacation when you feel like I do."

Tey came around the island so she could stand close enough to listen. Her bitterness did nothing to dampen her curiosity where Kendra was concerned.

"I'm sorry you're so miserable." It was hard to know what else to say when Kendra wasn't forthcoming about either her relationships or her emotions these days. It had been years since she'd told me the name of anyone she dated, let alone how she felt about them.

Luckily, my guess was right on the nose. "*Miserable* is exactly the right word," she said.

At my side, Teyana huffed. "She wouldn't know real misery if it bit her in the ass."

"Shh," I mouthed. God, I hated this. Hated the war between them. Hated not knowing how to push forward with my boss. Hated that I had an opportunity for our company and nothing I could do about it.

Except, I could do something about the last thing. "Hey, I'm glad you called," I said, making my decision to bring this up on a whim. "I had an opportunity come up for the company that I wanted to pass on. I was…" I paused, deciding how to dance around the truth. "At a party last night—friend of a friend of a friend—and I happened to meet someone there who works for the outreach division of Sebastian Industrial. He said they're looking to back a charity right now, and even gave me a contact so I could set up a meeting for you when—"

"No," she snapped. "No meeting. I am not pitching to Sebastian Industrial."

"Then let me do it. I know it might be uncomfortable for you since they're family friends, but since they asked for the hookup, and if I'm the one meeting with them, it's not like you're pushing anything on them they don't want."

She made a noise that sounded like a bit-back laugh. "You've never pitched before."

"Because you've never let me."

"I'm certainly not letting you pitch to the Sebastians on your first go around. That would be setting you up for disaster. I care too much about you to just feed you to the wolves like that."

"Care about you my ass," Tey whisper-hissed.

I gave her a stern look, and while I was suddenly wishing she wasn't there for this conversation, I also realized I wouldn't be charging on without her there to support me. "So then I'll put them off for six months or so. When you get back, you can show me the ropes—"

Kendra cut me off. "I said no, Tess. I said no last time you brought them up, I'm saying no now. What part of no is it that you aren't understanding?"

Now it wasn't just Teyana sneering. She was right— Kendra didn't deserve my loyalty.

Part of me wanted to hang up on her right then. But acting rashly would only feel good in the moment. "Wouldn't be doing my job if I didn't at least pass on the opportunity," I said with gritted teeth.

"You've done that now. Moving on. I called you for a reason. I'm getting a new bed. It's special order and won't be there for another three or four weeks. I gave them your number to arrange delivery. Make sure the old bed is disposed of, please."

That was something else Kendra always did after a big breakup—replaced her bed so she wouldn't have to deal with the "memories."

"What a waste of good furniture," Teyana said with disgust.

I was usually put-off by how she squandered her mon-ey as well, but right now I was focused on the other infor-mation she'd given. "Will do. So you're still planning to be gone for another month then?"

I could practically hear her eye roll. "I don't know, Tess. I'll be gone as long as it takes to figure out which one I want to break up with and which one gets to have me. These decisions take time. Hold on a sec, will you?"

I exchanged a look with Tey while Kendra had a muf-fled conversation with someone else. Did she realize how self-important she came off? It was cringeworthy.

It was only a handful of seconds before she returned. "Gotta go, Tess. My concierge is here to take me to my mud bath." She'd hung up before I even had a chance to say goodbye.

I frowned as I threw down my phone. It wasn't fair. Sure, Kendra's life had started out hard. She'd been three years old when her parents found her in an orphanage in South Korea while there for a philanthropic visit. But she didn't remember anything from then. All her memories were of the spoiled, first-class life she currently lived.

Meanwhile, Teyana was the smartest, most genuine person I knew. Her ambition was as big as her pockets were shallow. If it weren't for her illness, she'd have made it to where Kendra was, without any handouts. That's how amazing she was.

But here we were. Kendra lived like a princess, Teyana faced chronic physical limitations, and I was once again being pushed back down the ladder I so badly wanted to climb. *If I were at the top*, I thought not for the first time, *things would be different.* There was so much good I could do.

And if Kendra refused to help me, I'd just have to do it without her.

I could feel Teyana studying me. "You better be thinking what I think you're thinking, Tess Turani."

"I'm thinking it's going to be a late night," I said. Good or bad, my mind was made up. "I have a pitch presentation to prepare."

SIX

The following Friday, I rode the elevator to the twenty-seventh floor of the Sebastian Center. I was a mess of nerves. My mouth was dry, my skin sweaty. The butterflies in my stomach were so active I thought I might fly away.

Everything about this idea was wrong.

I regretted it as soon as I'd called to make the appointment Monday morning with Julie Sanchez. As promised, Green Eyes had informed her I'd be calling. She was ready for me with a meeting time already set aside, only it was for three weeks in the future. It was too far away. There was too much of a chance that Kendra would be back by then.

I knew I should have walked away then. An immediate roadblock did not bode well for the rest of the plan. But since I was already on the phone with the woman, it wasn't like I could just back out.

"We could wait until then," I'd said, thinking as fast as I could. "But I have an amazing opportunity for a partnership that I just know is going to be gone by then. I'd really hate for SIC to miss out."

Julie had put me on hold for several minutes. Just when I'd thought I should hang up and change my number, she returned to the line. "Friday at ten. Mr. Sebastian can give you thirty minutes."

So here I was, on my way to what was likely to be a total disaster.

Be confident, I told myself for the fiftieth time that morning. Teyana had told me it another hundred and fifty times before that. It was the only way I had a chance of selling this. The only way I had a chance of not coming across like a total fool.

But it was hard to be self-assured when nothing about me was *me*—my clothes, my shoes, and the briefcase I carried had been borrowed from Kendra's closet. Even my laptop had been one she'd purchased for me. Only the presentation on it was completely mine, and considering the fact that I'd never fully prepared one of these pitches on my own and had definitely never delivered one, I was finding it difficult to place any faith in it.

No. I could do this. I could *be* this. *You have to leap to land, Tess. So go ahead now and leap.*

By the time the doors opened at my floor, I had done a pretty decent job of composing myself. I threw my shoulders back, held my head high, and walked through the glass doors into the public relations office.

Then I saw the receptionist and froze.

It was Eden, the woman from the roof. The woman I'd watched Blue Eyes finger-bang and dismiss like yesterday's newspaper. She worked *here*?

Of course she did.

Because that was my luck and this was a ridiculous idea, and because she'd been at a party hosted by the Sebastians, so why the hell wouldn't I expect that she was part of their circle?

I almost turned around and left.

But she was already staring at me, a welcoming smile on her face, and I remembered suddenly that even though I'd witnessed her in a private moment, she hadn't seen me. All I had to do was keep my cool, and this would be fine. Everything would be fine.

"How may I help you?" she asked when I finally forced myself to cross the several yards to her desk.

"Yes, I have an appointment with Scott Sebastian." I managed to sound poised, which in turn made me *feel* poised. I glanced at the clock on the wall behind her. I'd hoped to be early, but it seemed I'd made it just in time. "Tess Turani with Conscience Connect. Ten a.m."

Her brows knit as she studied her screen. "Oh. There you are. You're not meeting with Scott; you're booked with Brett. He's waiting for you in the meeting room. I'll take you back there."

"Ah. Okay. Thanks." I waited for her to come around the desk then followed the clip-clip of her heels down the marble hallway, glad to be behind her so she couldn't see my confusion on my face. Julie had said my appointment was with Mr. Sebastian. Had something come up? Or maybe it had been Green Eyes' plan all along to pass me off to someone else. It was silly to expect that the man on top would have taken a meeting like this personally.

It didn't help settle my nerves, though. In fact, it increased my apprehension. It made me realize I didn't have any clue how this pitch would be vetted. I'd been hoping to tie this up as fast as possible, but if I wasn't meeting with the head honcho, it was probably unlikely that this Brett guy would be able to sign off on anything today. Would he be the one who would pass the information on to Scott? Or would I have to come back and pitch again? If it was the latter, how soon could that happen because time was not on my side.

Dread tickled at my chest as Eden ushered me into a meeting room. There were so many unknowns. So many ways this could fall apart. So many—

My panic turned to surprise as I came face-to-face with Green Eyes. "Hi!"

"Hi." The warmth in his greeting echoed mine.

I was really glad to see him. But also really baffled. Was he Scott Sebastian, the man in charge of PR or Brett, the man Eden said I'd be meeting?

"Is something wrong?" he asked, apparently reading the puzzlement on my face.

"I just..." I took him in. He was dressed in a tan suit that made his eyes look more brown than green and stood at the opposite end of a conference table—a small one, meant to accommodate four or five people at most. If he was Scott—and he had to be because he was a Sebastian, right? How many Sebastians were there in the same department?—then maybe we were going to be joined by more people shortly, including Brett. Or maybe Scott had scheduled me with Brett and then managed to make time for me himself.

Whatever had happened, he was here, and he was waiting for me to say something coherent. "I just didn't expect to be meeting with *you*," I said. "I figured you'd pass me off to someone else."

"Hope it's not a disappointment. I've been looking forward to seeing you again." He stepped toward me and held out his hand. "I don't think we were ever properly introduced. Brett Sebastian."

"Tess Turani." I took his hand as the pieces came together. *Brett.* So he wasn't Scott. He looked more like a Brett, actually. Then, was he not in charge? More likely, the website was outdated. "Good to formally meet you. And not a disappointment at all."

"Glad to hear it. I'm sorry I didn't get to see you again at the party Saturday. I looked for you later, after Adrienne Thorne finally left."

"You did?"

"I did." There was no mistaking what his intentions were with that statement. Especially since he still held my hand, much longer than he should have for a simple introduction between two people about to do business.

My stomach began to knot. He was attractive, yes. But I hadn't come here for a booty call, and I definitely hadn't come here to try to win his persuasion with feminine wiles. I wanted to climb the ladder on my own two feet, not on my back.

Before I had to decide how to handle his flirtation, Brett abruptly dropped my hand. "And that's as far as I'm going to go with that. I'm a firm believer that business and pleasure are not good bedfellows, and I'm very intent on conducting business with you. Perhaps there will be a time for pleasure later on."

"Thank you. And perhaps." I was relieved, and though I didn't feel the same spark now that I had when I'd been tipsy, I would consider a date with him when this was all over.

Unless, of course, this whole charade blew up in my face, which was still a very strong possibility.

Too late to worry about that now.

"Should we get started?" he asked.

"Yes. Of course."

He waited for me to sit before he unbuttoned his suit jacket and sat down across from me. His gaze settled on me intently. "You have the floor, Ms. Turani."

And, wow. Having the full attention of a Sebastian was more stressful than I'd imagined.

It was also more exciting.

It gave me a sudden shot of adrenaline. I'd landed an opportunity to sell to one of the most powerful men in the city. Now was my chance to prove I deserved it.

I opened my briefcase—Kendra's briefcase—and pulled out one of the booklets I'd had printed the day before. Since it was just the two of us, I decided to forgo the laptop. My PowerPoint was solid, but I knew I would do better on the pitch without all the bells and whistles. I needed to connect with him personally.

In fact, my whole presentation seemed overboard now. Suddenly, I knew my angle. "I put together a portfolio of all of the charities I thought might be suitable for SIC." I handed him a booklet. "Each of them are worthy and notable and would be a fine fit for a company as prestigious as yours. I'm happy to go over the pros and cons, walk you through what a partnership with each would look like. Or we can skip all that, and I can tell you why Sebastian Industrial would be making a huge mistake if they chose to team up with any charity other than the Dysautonomia Relief Foundation."

I hadn't stuttered or tripped over my words once. I was so nailing this.

Now all he had to do was tell me to skip all the bullshit and tell him more about the DRF, and I'd have this thing in the bag. My heart hammered in my chest as he flipped through the booklet, waiting for his response.

After a handful of eternal seconds, he looked up at me encouragingly. "I'm definitely curious about the latter. Unfortunately, there's a whole team to convince, and they'll probably want to hear about every single one of your charities in great detail before making a decision. I apologize in advance for how long and drawn-out they'll make it."

My stomach dropped. There was so much he'd said to be distressed about. I picked the first one to focus on first. "A team?"

"Just five others. They won't see anyone until they've been vetted, which is what we're supposedly doing now. Just a formality, really. And a chance for me to tell you what to expect during the process. This portfolio you've put together is right in line with what they'll need to see. If you have a slide presentation, I'd recommend that as well."

"Okay." I'd been thrown, but that didn't mean I still didn't have a handle on this. I forced myself to take a breath and pivot. I'd already been prepared for the possibility of meeting with a group to begin with. This was no big deal. "I do have a presentation. PowerPoint. Should I set that up now?" There was a TV screen on the wall, but I had a hard time imagining five other people around that small table with us. Maybe we'd move to a bigger conference room.

He returned his attention to the booklet. "No. I don't need to see it. Based on this, I'm sure it's fine." He glanced up at me and must have realized the misunderstanding from my expression. "Oh, you mean set up for the team. They won't be joining us today. We'll have to schedule something for that."

My mouth went dry. I'd had to push to get this meeting as quickly as I did. "How soon could we make that happen?"

"I think we can squeeze you in early next week. Julie mentioned that you thought this was time sensitive. I'm guessing that has to do with that charity you're pushing most?"

"Yeah. Um." *Pull yourself together.* "They're actively seeking a sponsor. I'd hate for you to miss the chance to work with them when I know they'd be a perfect fit."

He closed the booklet and clasped his hands together in front of him. "If it were up to just me, Tess, I'd say sign us up right now. I know we've just met, but I have a gut instinct for these things. Just flipping through your material, I can tell you know what you're selling. It's already much more organized than some of the other pitches I've heard recently."

I swallowed, trying to clear the ball in the back of my throat. "Thank you. I appreciate that."

"I mean it, too. I'm sorry I don't have any authority to make that happen."

His candidness gave me courage to return it. "Really? That just...that surprises me, I guess."

He looked at me strangely. "Oh, because of the name? Yeah, I get that a lot."

Wait. What?

"I'm one of the lesser Sebastians," he said in explanation. "Not a descendent of Irving. Ida, his sister, was my grandmother. I'm just a cousin. Much less powerful, much less formidable."

"Oh." Then, when I'd fully digested what he'd said, "Ohhhh." God, I was an idiot. I'd heard his last name and just assumed. I was even more stupid for not spending any time learning about the Sebastian family tree. This past week in preparation, I'd been so focused on researching the business itself, looking for the best ways to move into the future with the DRF, that I'd completely missed investigating its past.

I vowed to myself to do that before the next meeting.

And what was that last thing he'd said? "Formidable?"

He waved a dismissive hand. "I shouldn't have said that. I don't want you to worry needlessly about your presentation. You'll only have one of the greater Sebastians in the room, and he's not one of the ones who bites." He reconsidered. "At least, he doesn't bite too hard."

I was not soothed. I wasn't a fan of powerful men who bit at all.

Brett's gaze moved suddenly to something behind me. "Ah, here he is now, in fact." He stood up and addressed the person behind me. "Great timing. We were just talking about you."

The dread from before returned in a flood. I knew before I stood up, before I turned around. I could feel it on my skin, the way it felt charged, like a current running through my veins. I knew in my bones that it was him.

Somehow I made it to my feet. Somehow my knees didn't give out as I turned to him. Somehow I managed not to fall apart when my gaze met his ocean blues. They were even more devastating than I'd remembered.

He smiled, a smile so smooth it was hard to believe he even recognized me. Except he *did* recognize me. His mouth might have been able to keep the fact hidden, but his eyes fell on my face with heated familiarity. His eyes sparked with triumph.

And Brett was completely unaware. "Scott, this is Tess Turani. She's with the charity liaison organization."

I let Blue Eyes—Scott—take my hand in his. His grip was the same as Brett's, maybe a little firmer, but the effect he had on my body was entirely different. It was like being plugged in. Like one hundred and ten volts were running through our touch.

"Yes," he said, a faint grit in his tone. "When I heard you were meeting with Conscience Connect today, I decided I had to stop by and see who your contact was since I knew there was no way Kendra would reach out herself.

Nice to officially meet you, Tess...Turani, was it?"

"Uh-huh." It was the only sound I was capable of producing. I'd slept with him. And now I was going to have to work with him. And he was a Sebastian.

"There are several of them around here," he'd said when I brought up the name at the party.

I wanted to hit myself.

And he knew Kendra! The mystery man who'd given me the best sex in my life was here and he was a Sebastian and he was the man in charge, and he fucking knew Kendra.

"Thank you, Brett," he said, his hand still clutching mine. "I can take this from here. Could you shut the door on the way out?"

"Oh. Sure. No problem." Brett seemed surprised at being dismissed. But he was a lesser Sebastian, as he'd said, and there was no way he was going to refute it. Halfway out the room, he did turn back. "Tess, I'll have Julie call the number on file to set up that meeting for next week, if that works?"

With my eyes still locked on Scott, I cleared my throat. "Yes. Please. Thank you, Brett."

Then the door was shut, and it was just me and Scott.

"Looks like I found you," he said with a wicked smirk.

Yep. I was totally doomed.

SEVEN

"Looks like you found me," I said, echoing Scott. Because holy shit, the flags had been there, and I'd missed every one. He'd been at that party. His car and apartment were state-of-the-art luxury. I hadn't bothered to check out his name. I was a first-class idiot. I hadn't just walked into the lion's den. I'd come in blazing.

What the hell was I supposed to do now?

Meanwhile, Scott's smirk remained as he dropped my hand and circled around me, tracing my body with his blue eyes, taking every speck of me in. It was the kind of greedy, possessive, curious look that I would have found highly inappropriate under any other circumstance. Not that it wasn't inappropriate now too—even more so considering the power dynamic—just, I was finding it hard to mind.

I was so over my head, it was amazing I could still breathe.

"So. You're a Sebastian," I said when it was obvious he was enjoying the upper hand too much to risk giving anything away without prodding.

His smirk morphed into a smug smile. "One of many."

A beat passed. A beat in which I replayed the conversation at the bar once again. He'd heard me going on and on about meeting a Sebastian. He had to have realized how easily he could have won me over by simply dropping his own name. "Why didn't you tell me?"

"You said no names."

"You had an opportunity to tell me before that. I would have thought you would jump all over telling me when I showed interest in the family."

He gave a one-shoulder shrug. "I was afraid you'd go home with me if I told you."

"Wasn't that what you'd wanted?"

"Wanted you to go home with me, yes. I didn't want that to be the reason."

That shut me up. There was a hint of vulnerability to his words that surprised me. Made me feel embarrassed for my excitement about meeting someone just because they were famously rich. I'd often been critical about how rarely the upper class mixed themselves with the rest of us, calling them snooty and self-absorbed. I hadn't ever considered there might be another side to the separation.

"I'm sorry I made you feel like you had to be guarded," I said after a beat. Then I kicked myself for it because that was what I was concerned with right now? When there was so much on the line for me?

"Don't," he said. "No apologies for that. That was a me thing, not a Tessa Turani thing." His lip turned up after saying my name, like it was a sound that gave him pleasure to make. "Tessa Turani," he repeated, going back for a second taste.

The way his tongue wrapped around the *ss* made me remember his tongue on my body. Made my heart race and every neuron in my body fire.

None of which was convenient when I was trying to establish myself as a professional.

"It's Tess," I snapped, trying to gain some sort of balance.

"I like Tessa," he said with a finality that made me unable to argue. He unbuttoned his suit jacket and half sat, half leaned on the table, a very casual posture that did nothing to diminish his looming presence. "Kendra finally decided to pitch us, huh? Interesting."

My stomach turned to a rock at the mention of Kendra. It occurred to me now that there might have been more to her refusal to present to SIC. How well did Scott know Kendra?

It seemed like he was waiting for me to say something. I chose the most benign thing I could think of. "She did say the Sebastians were family friends."

"Family friends. Yes." He seemed to find the term amusing. "The Montgomerys and the Sebastians go way back. I suppose that's why she sent you instead of reaching out herself?"

Oh, God. There was history.

A history that I couldn't guess at if I tried. Best thing to do was keep playing the uninformed employee. "Probably so. And she's out of town. So I'm doing all her pitches in her place." It could be possible.

I just had to pray that Scott and Kendra weren't close enough that he would know she'd never let anyone do anything in her place.

He considered that for several seconds while I held my breath and hoped he couldn't hear the knocking of my knees and tried not to stare too intently at the perfection of his angular jawline.

"Well, I'm glad she wants to work with us," he said finally. "There shouldn't be any reason our family relationship should stand in the way of making great things happen."

"I'm sure she feels the same," I said, wary that this was too easy.

He nodded once. "She's out of town?"

I was suspicious about his reason for asking. But even if he was planning on trying to contact her, he wouldn't be successful. For once I thanked God for Kendra's flair for the dramatic. "Completely off the grid. No phone, no social media. She calls me occasionally to check in, but she isn't using her own cell when she does."

"Sounds enviable. Any idea when she'll be back?"

"A couple of weeks? Maybe a couple of months." There was no use lying about it. I was already coming to terms that I'd probably lose my job over this. Hopefully, I could seal up a partnership with Sebastian Industrial and the DRF before I had to accept their employment offer.

"Think we can have all this business wrapped up before that?"

Instead of wondering why he was so eager to get things done, I focused on the possibility that the universe was, for once, on my side. "It's completely doable if SIC makes it a priority."

Again, a nod of his head. "The presentation to the team is next, correct? What's the process from there?" He picked up the booklet I'd given Brett that got left behind in his hasty departure and leafed through it.

I blinked as I pivoted to full-on business mode. "I'll talk in depth about the organizations that I think would be the best candidates for sponsorship. As soon as you select one, I'll invite them to sit in on a coordination meeting. We've never had a charity turn down an offer, so from there, it's pretty much a done deal. Really, the speed of the process depends on how quickly you can make a decision."

"And then when the deal is done, you're no longer involved?"

"Well." I couldn't tell if he was trying to get rid of me or prolong our working together. I needed it to be the former. I hated how much I wished it were the latter.

The smart thing would be to craft an answer that would ensure he was on my side, but not knowing his motives, I had to stick with the facts. "It varies based on the contract. Conscience Connect will continue to be a liaison during the initial phase, for sure. After that, the charity will generally fill that position with someone on their own team." Me, possibly. If they chose the DRF, and if I ended up working for them.

"And your salary comes out of the sponsorship funds? You don't get paid until then."

"Conscience Connect gets paid when the check clears."

"Another reason to get this moving along."

My muscles relaxed with relief. He was looking out for my paycheck, that was all. Too bad it was one I'd never directly receive. If it was a really good paycheck though, maybe it would be enough to convince Kendra to let me keep my job in the end. With a bonus even. Or, better yet, a raise.

But I was getting ahead of myself. "I'd appreciate that."

He stood and buttoned his jacket, tucking the booklet I'd made under his arm. "I believe the team already has a meeting on the schedule for Monday. I'll have the agenda cleared so you can present to us then."

"Okay. Thank you."

His eyes met mine, a collision that made me dizzy. He held out his hand to shake, and when I gave him mine, an electric shock went through my body, big enough to wake me up to the fact that I wasn't just getting ahead of myself, I was also batshit crazy because how the hell did I think I could work with a man who I'd slept with? A man who had this much power over me. A man who could easily turn on the charm, and I'd be giving him my panties in a blink.

Though, except for his initial flirtation, he'd been completely professional.

I extricated my hand from his and looked at him sideways. "We aren't going to be a problem, are we?"

"Why would we be?" He stuffed his hands in his suit pockets, completely casual. As though nothing had happened between us.

"Because of the other night," I deadpanned.

"What about it?"

Oh, right. He was the guy who made a girl *say it*. I knew this game. The fact he was making me play it didn't bode well for this arrangement.

All the more reason why this had to be addressed now.

I crossed my arms over my chest. "We had sex, Scott."

"Oral sex."

"Right." Mind-bending oral sex. And why would he point that out if... "What?"

"Wait." His grin was slow like he was savoring the thought behind it. "You didn't think that we...?"

Oh my God.

We hadn't…?

But I thought...

My cheeks felt so hot that I was sure they were red, despite the fact that they didn't show color easily. How had I gotten this so humiliatingly wrong?

And Scott was enjoying every second of it, according to the smirk on his face.

No. I'd had valid reasons for thinking what I'd thought. "I woke up naked. In your bed. After what had happened in the car. I made the obvious assumption."

His smile vanished. "Oh hold up. That is offensive, Tessa, on so many levels. I think I proved myself a gentleman. Presuming I couldn't undress you and put you to bed and behave myself is insulting."

I opened my mouth to respond, but he went on before I could. "More insulting is that you think you could forget fucking me. You wouldn't. No matter how inebriated you were. You wouldn't have been able to leave the bed that morning. Certainly not without nourishment, and even then you would be hobbling."

"You are really full of yourself."

He ignored me. "Most insulting is that you think I'd fuck a woman that drunk. I am not completely morally depraved."

I was not going to apologize for my assumptions. "Why isn't that a natural conclusion? Any woman would assume that if they'd woken up in your bed. Especially when they couldn't remember getting there. And after you'd already...you know." I wasn't going to give him the satisfaction of saying it again.

He was more than ready to fill in the blank for me. "Devoured your pussy? Yes. I did do that. You were saying, yes, yes, yes but it occurred to me while that was going on that you might not be capable of consent."

"I came three times."

He winked. "Like I said, I'm unforgettable."

"That wasn't what I..." Why was it so hard to focus when he was standing near me? And when had he moved so close? I took a step backward. "My point is that it took you long enough to consider consent."

"Yes." He feigned a sigh. "It should have occurred to me earlier, I admit. I'd like to say I lost restraint because I was drinking as well—which is true—but also I went down on you because I really wanted to, and I have a hard time resisting what I want. Especially when it's right in front of me." And now, somehow, he was up close again. "Do you want to file a complaint of assault?"

"What? No. That's ludicrous. I was begging you." He smelled so good, I wasn't far from begging him now too.

My chin was lifted, my nostrils flared from taking in his manly scent, when I caught myself. This was not a good idea. *He* was not a good idea.

I took two steps back this time, hoping that would diffuse the energy between us. Praying that I could make myself say something smart and proper and put an end to all the naughty thoughts suddenly swimming in my head.

"I was drunk," I said. "I don't fault you for anything that happened. I'm sorry I'd assumed it was more. If I had been more with it, I'm sure it would have been. Consensually so. It was a fun time. But I'm not that woman on the regular."

His jaw ticked. His eyes sparked. "Do you want to be?"

"Uh...what?"

"We're not drunk now."

"Oh. Oh." I should have been saying no, no. Not just to his suggestion, but to working with him all together. I was not a strong enough woman to resist a man as ridiculously bad for me as Scott Sebastian was.

I spun away from him and took a deep breath. When I wasn't facing him, I felt more resilient. "There can't be anything between us, Scott. It's unprofessional and inappropriate." I turned back toward him. "And because we're not drunk now, I'm not so reticent to consider filing a complaint if you make a suggestion like that again."

That seemed to bring him to his senses. "We don't need to go there. I'm not trying to be inappropriate. Put all of this aside. Also, let me be clear, I'm not going to oust you from this project because of anything you say or do or don't say or don't do. I don't want you to feel like there's a power dynamic at play here. I'm not your boss. I'm the guy on the rooftop. You're the hot girl with the mesmerizing eyes, and I just want to spend time with you." His expression was sincere when he added, "Preferably sober and fucking."

Why, why, why did he have to be so irresistible?

And how could he possibly believe there was no power dynamic between us?

I ran my hand over my face in frustration. "You can't do that, you realize. You can't just 'put all of this aside.' Our situation doesn't go away just because you pretend it doesn't exist. Not for me. You're still you. You still hold the power. You get that, right?"

"Yes, I get that I'm a Sebastian and that there are advantages associated with that." His tone was also frustrated. Then it softened into something more vulnerable but equally intense. "But what good is power if it doesn't get you what you want?"

Smooth. So fucking smooth.

Smooth enough to overcome the rough front I was trying to put on. He could have me. I was weak. I was willing.

But before I could close the distance and throw myself in his arms like I so very much wanted to, he backed away, his hands up in surrender. "You're right. I crossed the line. I apologize. You're here to do a job. I'll let you do it without harassment. I'll have my assistant or Julie give you a call with that meeting time on Monday. Thank you for coming by, Ms. Turani. I'm sure you can find your way out. You've proven yourself good at that."

He left me gaping and alone and incredibly disappointed that I didn't feel more relieved.

EIGHT

When Teyana came over later that afternoon, she found me lying on the floor in Kendra's closet. "It went that bad?"

I moved my arm from where it had been draped over my eye to look at her. "It didn't go well."

She nodded thoughtfully, likely trying to decide how much of my reaction to the meeting at SIC was real and how much was dramatics. "This position is a familiar one for me. I don't usually do it in the closet though."

"You've never had a closet big enough."

"Good point. But was there a reason you chose the closet?"

I grimaced as I remembered how I'd arrived here. "I came in to choose something to wear for my next meeting. Then I started thinking about all the money I'm going to need to pay the dry-cleaning bill for all the outfits I've been borrowing, and I suddenly needed to lie down."

Her eyes brightened at the hint of a "next meeting," but like a good friend, she zoned in on the problem at hand. "Don't dry-clean. Hang them back up, and don't say a word."

"I can't be in a room with those people and not be nervous. And I sweat."

"You're saving on commute money, and we'll cook instead of ordering out."

"Fine," I sighed. This was where I was being dramatic. I lived paycheck to paycheck, but I had non-essentials in my budget. "You're right."

"Mmhmm." She gave me a superior smirk as she dropped her overnight bag and leaned her cane against the shelf.

"How are you feeling today?" I asked belatedly. It should have been my first question. A trip into the city was always exhausting for her, but she'd insisted on coming.

"Feeling pretty great, actually."

"That makes me happy."

She lived for these days, when her energy matched her ambition, and she got to "live" instead of just exist. We both knew she'd feel it tomorrow. It was a good thing she was spending the weekend with me instead of going back to Jersey City tonight.

"Hang on," she said, squatting beside me. "Let me get down there with you, and you can tell me all about it."

I waited until she was prone and comfortable to begin. Then I spent the next half hour detailing the entire morning, starting with finding Eden at the welcome desk and ending with Scott Sebastian leaving me wound up in the meeting room.

"I think after all that, I'd be lying on the floor in the

closet too," she said when I'd finished.

"You are lying on the floor in the closet too," I pointed out.

My smile faded fast, though. Retelling the events had returned my focus to the mess I was in and the anxiety that sat like a medicine ball in my stomach. I let out a groan. "What am I going to do, Tey?"

She turned toward me, bringing her knees into her chest and propping her head up on her hand. "What do you want to do?"

"Well, I don't want to get fired, but obviously that's on the horizon." In some ways, accepting that made my decisions easier. There was no reason to bail if I was going to face Kendra's wrath no matter what. "I guess what I want is to make sure SIC picks the Dysautonomia Relief Foundation as their charity. That's the only good that can come out of this."

"That's a bunch of baloney. There are other fantastic charities in your portfolio. Anything they pick will be for the good."

I narrowed my eyes at her. "I get what you're doing, Teyana Lewis, managing my expectations and all. But I want it to be the DRF. I'm going to sell them the DRF." Saying it that emphatically felt like making a promise. It was a promise I would work my ass off to keep.

"I hope you aren't just doing that for me." She blinked, obviously touched.

"Well. A little. But also for me. If I can sell the DRF, then maybe I can negotiate a better salary than the one Sarah previously offered. And I need to have a reason for them to hire me in case the offer has expired or something."

"Ooh. Good call."

A fraction of my anxiety lifted. I was sure I'd thought through the entire situation, inside and out, but I was grateful for the validation.

"I haven't reached out to Sarah about proposing this yet either. Don't want to get her hopes up. I'll call her when SIC invites her for the consultation meeting."

"Then you've decided what you're doing. You got this. Easy peasy lemon squeezy." When Teyana believed in me, it was so much easier to believe in myself.

Still, I wasn't done freaking out. And with her here and on my side, I could now fully let myself worry. I sat up and twisted so I was facing her, my back against the shelves full of Kendra's extensive assortment of purses. "But what if they don't choose the DRF?"

"Then you sell them something else and Sarah will still hire you. She's said before she knows you're going to accept eventually. She's just waiting for you to know it too."

Yes, I'd have a job somewhere. I supposed I wasn't concerned about that. "What if Kendra shows up before the deal is done?"

She shrugged. "Then she finishes it up. She can't walk away once it's started."

Humiliating, but survivable. "What if Scott calls Kendra and finds out I'm a sham before this really gets anywhere?"

Tey sat up for this one. "Number A," she said, pointing a single finger. "She's never going to answer her phone." She put up a second finger. "Number B, same results as if she showed up. You go work for the DRF. This is a no-lose situation, baby."

"But he could hate me," I whispered.

"Scott? Yeah, I suppose there's that." Even Tey couldn't spin that into a comforting lie.

I shook my head in self-irritation, the shelf digging into my neck as I did. It was ridiculous that I cared about what Scott Sebastian thought of me, but I did. More than I wanted to admit.

A beat passed before Tey spoke again. "Do you think he fucked Kendra?"

"Oh my God, I'm trying not to go there!" It was the thought I'd somehow managed to push off until now. Once invited, the image rushed into my head, graphic and disturbing.

"But you're looking at the worst possibilities, right? Which means you need to go there. It's irresponsible not to. So what if he did?"

I scowled at her, convinced the question was more about needling out my feelings than it was about responsibility. "Then I'd be jealous," I admitted. I was jealous just thinking about the possibility. It was stupid because I hadn't felt that way as much about Eden, who I knew had fucked around with Scott. Probably because of Kendra. Because I knew her. Because she always got what she wanted and never appreciated it.

God, what was wrong with me? The guy wasn't even mine.

"I get it," Tey said, as if she could read my thoughts. "Besides the icky feelings, what's the worst thing that it would mean in terms of the job?"

Maybe I'd been wrong about her motives. Now that I thought about it, there was an advantage to asking this question. "It probably helps the situation, honestly. Typical Kendra, she'll never talk to him again. I kind of think that's his M.O. as well."

"He does seem like the heartbreaker type."

"You only know him from what I've told you."

"You've painted a very clear picture."

I attempted a laugh. It was hard to think there was a silver lining to the very real possibility that my boss had slept with the hottest man I'd ever met. A hot man who'd also shown interest in me. "He did hit on me again after our night together."

She understood my concern. "But nothing actually happened. You're different. You're still the unknown."

That was something else I hadn't let myself think about—the sex that we didn't have. On the one hand, I was glad not to have missed something that was surely mind-blowing. It also made it easier to keep this strictly business. On the other hand, it made me feel like I didn't actually own a thing that I'd thought I'd owned. A thing that Kendra might have owned. Now I wanted to own it more than I did when I'd supposedly owned it.

"Is it a good thing or a bad thing that I didn't sleep with him?" I asked, wanting to figure out how to feel about this bit of information.

"It's neither," Tey said matter-of-factly. "It's just a thing. It's why he won't try to call Kendra, and why he will try to call you." She paused before asking the question we both knew she needed to ask next. "What will you do when he tries to bed you again?"

Not if. When. She was that certain it would happen.

Why did I feel such an overwhelming adrenaline rush at the thought of it? "I don't know the answer to that one, Tey." I knew what I should do. But I also knew myself, knew just how weak I was around men like Scott Sebastian.

Tey looked at me with wide-eyed shock. "You can't sleep with him, Tess! You absolutely cannot, no matter how much he makes your snatch tingle. That is not how you want this to go down."

She let the lecture sink in, and when she spoke again it was less stern. "Look, you go in there, you pitch this deal, sign the contracts, seal up a job at the DRF. Then you can bang his brains out."

He'd likely find out I was a fraud before then, which completely erased any possibility of the fantasy becoming reality.

Ignoring that fact, though, I nodded in agreement. "Sounds like a real good plan."

"Are you ready for this?" Brett asked quietly as the team members arrived at the SIC conference room.

My heart pounded furiously as I considered my answer. Sure, I was ready for this. My presentation was solid. The PowerPoint was hooked up and ready to go. My handouts were already placed around the table. I had both a water bottle and a cup of coffee. On top of that, I looked pretty damn good in the Oscar de la Renta printed blouse and pants I'd stolen from Kendra's wardrobe.

But was I *ready* for this? Not fucking ready at all.

"My hands are so clammy, I'm afraid to shake anyone's hands," I said, which told him all he needed to know.

"Stay back here as they come in. I'll intro you when they're all seated, and there will be no need for shaking." But he knew what I was really saying. "You're going to be amazing, Tess. You got this."

"Thank you." I knew he meant well, but his words didn't do anything to calm my nerves. His faith in me was purely speculation since he hadn't actually seen my presentation, and considering this was not only the first time I'd be pitching to this group, but also the first time I was pitching ever, I really could have used a pep talk that was based on first-hand knowledge.

I looked at the people sitting around the room, immersed in workplace banter. Two women, three men, and a spot for Brett. The chair at the opposite end of the table remained empty. I swallowed when I thought about the man who'd soon be sitting there.

"Silvia, Paris, Matthew M., Matthew T.—he's the one we call Matt. Anthony's the one with the sparkling water." Brett pointed them all out discreetly. "It's an easy crowd. Except for Scott, but you've already met him."

There was a hint of a question in the last statement, an invitation for me to explain exactly how well I knew Scott. Even if I wanted to share that with Brett, it was something

I was trying very hard not to think about at the moment.

Besides, I was too hung up on his implication. "Scott's difficult?"

I could tell he was torn between honesty and not wanting to intimidate me more. "Well, yeah. I mean, the Greater Sebastians have a reputation for a reason. At least he's not one of Reynard's sons. That stem of the family is brutal."

Nothing he said was comforting.

My expression must have exposed my terror. He picked up my cell from the table where he'd placed it so I could keep tabs on the time. "Here, unlock your phone," he said, as he'd said that first night we met. When I handed it back to him, he typed in a new contact then sent a message to the new number. "That's me. You can slip in a text if you need me. I'll ping you if you run off track, which you won't. Does that help?"

It did. Except the room had abruptly gone quiet, and when I looked up, Scott was striding to his seat at the head of the table. He was devastating in his dark gray suit, his expression severe, and if I wasn't imagining it, he was glaring at me and Brett.

Yeah, I didn't feel better at all.

That wasn't exactly true. My skin buzzed, my nipples perked. My blood hummed. My heart felt like it might pound its way out of my chest, but other than that, my body seemed to really like it when Scott Sebastian was near.

Stupid body.

I took my phone back from Brett who scurried to attention like a student tardy for class. I glanced around the room and found everyone's eyes on Scott, so I placed mine there too, even though doing so made my chest feel tight. They would have ended up there on their own eventually anyway. He was magnetic. He drew my gaze whether I wanted to give it to him or not.

I hated how much I wanted him to give me his gaze in return.

But other than the scowl he'd delivered as he walked in, he didn't pay me any notice at all.

"Today's agenda has been amended," he said to the team. "We're still discussing possible sponsorship opportunities, of course. Conscience Connect has decided to help us with the process. I'll turn it over to Brett to introduce the liaison." He looked at his watch. "Let's stay on task, please. I have somewhere to be at four."

I tried not to be disappointed about his lack of regard. Tried not to care that I only had one hour of his precious time. Tried hardest not to think about how sexy he made the simple act of glancing at the time.

It was easy enough to push all those distractions away when Brett began his introduction and Scott finally did swing his attention toward me, and I saw nothing but cold indifference.

So much for worrying about our chemistry. The man was obviously over me. I'd known this was who he was from minute one, and still it was a wound to my pride. I had a sudden sympathy for Eden and the way he'd dismissed her that night on the roof. What was it about girls like us who recognized the player and still insisted on being played?

At least it made this less complicated. All the more incentive to get this deal done as fast as I could.

And I would do it like a pro, with my head held high, and my presentation on point.

As soon as Brett finished explaining how Conscience Connect worked and made my introduction, I jumped into my pitch. I had eight charities to introduce. I planned on devoting no more than five minutes to each of the first seven which would leave more than twenty minutes to push the DRF and to answer any questions. I had this in the bag. I'd practiced and timed it out several times to be sure.

Unfortunately, when I'd practiced, I hadn't accounted for all the interruptions. Detailed questions that were irrelevant at this early point, such as demographic breakdowns of a charity's disbursements and how previous sponsors had gone about promoting the organization.

I would have explained that those questions were best saved for when we'd narrowed down the choices or at least asked that they be held until the end to be answered if it hadn't been Scott who was asking.

Every time.

Every single goddamn interruption came from Scott.

I didn't have to text Brett to know that it wasn't a good idea to argue with the man in charge. So there was nothing I could do about it but let him steer us off course. It was exasperating how it happened. How I'd just start to get my stride when he'd cut in with a question. I'd fumble to come up with the answer. Quickly he'd shoot back something that concerned him about whatever I'd said. Then it would open the door for the team to jump in, and Scott would sit back and smile smugly while everything spiraled out of control.

"They had that awful float in the Macy's parade last year," Matt would say. "Do you think they'd let us have some input on that?"

Brett would try to help as much as he could. "That's probably not something we need to be discussing at this point."

"It most certainly is," Silvia would disagree. "We need to know how willing they'd be to adjust to our brand before we even consider working with a company."

And so it went. I could hardly get through one slide before the diversions would start. Twenty-five minutes in, I was just moving to the second charity. While Anthony and Paris argued about the relevance of a newly founded charity versus an older one, I checked the time and panicked. There was also a text notification from Brett.

> Don't worry. You're doing fine. This is par for the course.

I looked up from my screen to see Scott glaring at the phone in my hand then down at the phone in front of Brett. Maybe he was a no-cells-at-work kind of guy. I hurriedly turned it on its face and didn't check it again.

Even without the clock, I knew I had to start cutting things short. If I could quickly get through the second, I decided, I'd skip to the DRF and hit it hard. I sped through my script, and despite the continued interruptions, I managed to feel like I was making progress when I wrapped it up and flipped forward through my slides.

"I'm going to change direction here and jump to the charity that I really think is best suited—"

That was as far as I got before Scott cut me off. "I think this is a good time to break for today."

"But I still have six charities to present!" I exclaimed, in a much less professional tone than I would have liked. Then, getting a handle on myself, I said, "Is it already four?"

"It's about eight to," Scott said, without checking his watch. "Certainly not enough time to move on to another charity. I already feel we've rushed this as is."

This was rushed?

"Here's what we'll do," he continued. "We'll meet each day this week for a working lunch and go over one charity each session. In fact, let's start with the two we went over today in tomorrow's meeting. I feel like there is plenty we didn't touch on that should be considered before moving to the next vetting stage."

He didn't ask if anyone had any conflicts. Didn't ask if *I* had any conflicts, and I wasn't even his employee. He just made the declaration, and while there were some words muttered under the breath of some of the team members, not-a-one of them protested. They just pulled out their devices and entered the new information in.

In other circumstances, his ability to command would have been super fucking hot.

In these circumstances, I was too distracted by my dread. I wouldn't get through these until the middle of next week at this rate. And then there'd be a next stage of vetting? My stomach felt like it was reaching for the floor.

If he hadn't told me he wanted this completed before Kendra came back, I would have sworn he was dragging this out on purpose. And what point would he have in doing that?

I considered cornering him to remind him of the rush goal, but he was out of the room before I could take a step. Without any sort of acknowledgement. Without so much as a glance in my direction.

That almost bothered me the most.

"Is that workable with your schedule?" Brett asked as the others cleared up their belongings and made their way out of the room. At least he had some sense of courtesy.

"If it wasn't, would it matter?"

He smiled sympathetically. "You're free to object. You have no obligation to do things on his timeline."

I heard what he didn't say—if I *did* object, I might lose the contract. No wonder Brett had called him difficult.

Then again, Scott hadn't been obligated to give me the time that he had. If he was always this thorough, he could have spaced these meetings out for months. Instead, he'd given me every day of the week.

"I can make it," I said to Brett. Because I had the time, and I wanted the job. Not at all because I hoped that Scott Sebastian had just done me a favor.

NINE

The meetings didn't get any better from there. Each dragged on as the team dissected every facet of the day's proposed charity. Each time, the dissection was led by a man I was truly beginning to think of as an enemy. I wasn't giving a presentation so much as leading a discussion, and I certainly wasn't in charge, so I no longer stood. Instead, I sat at one end of the oval conference table, directly across from Scott, and hoped it was far enough away that he couldn't feel the extent of my loathing.

The worst part of it all was that I was certain I'd feel completely different about the whole thing if Scott looked at me like I was more than a representative of Conscience Connect.

Which meant I wasn't only hating him but also myself. Why did I even care? So he was stupid hot, insanely rich, and knew how to use his tongue. That didn't mean his opinion mattered.

Of course his opinion *did* matter. Because he was the one in charge. Because he was the one who would ultimately decide how this whole charade played out. Because I *was* a representative for Conscience Connect.

I just rarely had business in mind when I sat longing for his attention.

By Thursday, the longing and the hating and the boredom made me feel like I was about to burst out of my skin. The hour was already up, and I'd yet to get through my first page of notes about the Environment Conservation Fund. The discussion had gotten wildly off task, and to top it all off, Scott had spent most of the lunch stabbing at his phone.

He was a busy man, I reminded myself. He could be making lucrative trades or handling a PR crisis. He could also be playing *Clash of Clans*, and no one would be the wiser.

Unfortunately, I was in a mood that assumed the worst, but even my best shot eye-daggers didn't pull his head up from the screen.

With a sigh, I tried to turn my focus back to the discussion.

"I don't know why it matters what percentage of their funds are spent in the States versus globally," Silvia was saying. "Environmental concerns are worldwide."

"Because we're primarily based in the U.S.," Matthew argued. "And if we're taking on a sponsorship in order to boost our image with people in the U.S., it definitely matters that the charity appeals to people in the U.S."

"Don't people who care about the environment care about it as a whole?" Paris asked.

I didn't hear who answered or what they said because

suddenly the only thing I was aware of was how close Eden was standing next to Scott as she refilled his coffee.

Like, ridiculously close. I was ninety-nine point nine percent certain her arm was pressed against his back.

It made me more happy than it should that he didn't look up from his phone for her either.

God, I was so petty. I didn't own him in any way. In fact, she probably had more of a rightful claim on him than I did, considering what I'd witnessed on the roof. It wasn't her fault that she was attracted to an absolutely breathtaking man-whore. I couldn't resent her for wanting whatever he'd give. For wanting it so badly, she'd steal it as she served him unnoticed.

I related way more than was healthy.

I was also raised in a society that pitted women against each other when a man was involved, and though I wanted to be someone who could rise above that, I was also human.

I picked up my phone and sent a text.

What's the deal with Eden and Scott?

Brett's phone vibrated in front of him. He shot a glance at his boss before picking it up, a habit probably so drilled into him that he might not have even been conscious of it. He considered for several seconds before typing anything.

Why do you ask?

His suspicious answer reminded me that Brett had a bit of a crush on me. I'd have been an idiot not to notice his frequent and prolonged stares and the banter that bordered on flirting. Plus, he'd basically stated his interest at our first interview.

The man was admittedly attractive. Enough so that I might have found myself in his bed, if the situation at the party had gone differently.

But he wasn't Scott.

He didn't make my heart trip or my skin burn. He didn't make the space between my legs pulse. He didn't steal my gaze every time he walked in the room.

Not that I'd ever let on to Brett. Especially because I suspected he had a bit of an inferiority complex where Scott was concerned, and the last thing I wanted to do was hurt his feelings with my catty jealousy.

> Because office gossip is more inter-esting than the dumpster fire going on around us, and she's obviously into him. So spill the tea.

> His reply was quicker after that. She's into him.

I glared at him down the table, giving him a look that said, *Is that all you got?*

> He chuckled then typed more. He dicks her over like he dicks every woman. She keeps going back. Not sure what she sees in the guy, honestly. He's just go-ing to keep breaking her heart.

I was impressed Brett knew that much about the situation. I wondered if it was common knowledge, or if he had a vested interest. Did Brett possibly have eyes for Eden as well?

The sound of a throat clearing loudly and pointedly drew my eyes up from the screen and smack into Scott's scornful scowl. Instantly, I put the phone down and my hands in my lap and tried to hide any guilt from my expression. *I could have been just as busy as you were, buddy.*

But Scott's scowl darted to Brett, and it was evident he knew exactly what was going on.

He opened his mouth, and I prepared to be lectured. Well, I'd wanted his attention, hadn't I?

But when he spoke, it wasn't about me. "We have a global presence. Our charity should have a global presence as well. Having said that, we aren't going with an environmental cause. Too political. My father would never support that."

It threw me to think that there was someone higher up than Scott Sebastian. He carried himself like he was the man on top. I couldn't imagine how much more commanding his father had to be.

I might have dwelled on that more if Eden wasn't currently bending over to whisper something in Scott's ear and if the other thing he'd said hadn't just pissed me the fuck off. "You knew all along that an environmental cause was ineligible, and yet you let me spend this entire hour presenting a foundation that's entire mission is to help the environment?"

The normally restless room went still. I probably should have tried harder to hide my irritation.

Scott frowned, and I got giddy because something I'd said had impacted him enough to have a reaction. Didn't even care that it was a negative one.

Then I realized the frown was for Eden and whatever she'd said to him. "I'll call him later. He can wait." She scurried off to deliver his message, and he turned his focus to my outburst. "You'd already done the prep. I didn't want that time to go to waste."

His inability to see the irony in his statement was maddening. Time was against me. I didn't have the luxury of spending a single minute discussing any charity that wasn't a viable partner, and here I'd spent fifty-two minutes doing just that.

The only thing that kept me from going full-out Vesuvius and exploding was the realization that he'd done me another favor. "I'm glad I know now. I'll cut the other two environmental charities outlined in the booklet. That means we only have four more instead of six."

"Good call," he said. I felt the *but* coming before he said it. "Since we already have the time dedicated to it, you can replace them with two other options."

While I'd never seen Kendra give one of these presentations, I knew what she'd do. She'd put on that winning smile of hers. She'd agree to whatever was asked. She'd do the dance. Then she'd complain and rant about them later behind their back as all professionals should.

But I wasn't Kendra. And, no matter how much I wanted to be professional, my patience had been worn thin. "There really is no reason to do that," I said, pouring on as much sugar to my tone as I could muster. "I've already pulled the top eight charities seeking big sponsors. Anything else I'd show you would be subpar."

"By your standards." The condescension in his tone was evident.

In my periphery, I saw a text message flash across my phone screen. I didn't have to look at it or at Brett holding his own cell to know it was from him. A warning, probably. *Step down, Tess.*

I didn't step down. "Yes, Mr. Sebastian. By my standards. But that's my job here. To use my knowledge to narrow down the cream of the crop. If you don't trust my expertise, then I don't know what we're even doing here."

I smiled as I spoke, still my words came out clipped, and when I'd finished speaking, I could feel everyone's eyes move from me to him, waiting for him to counter.

He didn't bother with a smile. "It's also your job to give us a sufficient number of charities to choose from. You indicated we'd see eight charities. I expect to see eight charities."

"And I expected to be given parameters before I wasted my time delivering a pitch that you weren't even planning to consider. Or perhaps you didn't realize I was even talking about the environment today until the entire hour had passed because you were too wrapped up in your goddamn phone."

Now he smiled, when the tension in the room had reached a peak, the kind of smile that could only be delivered by someone who held all the cards. Someone who had nothing to lose.

"We're done here today," he said, the control in his

voice a stark contrast to the rage that had been in mine. Too cool to be anything but unnerving. "Tess, we'll discuss this in my office."

Not Tessa.

That he hadn't used his preferred name for me disappointed me almost as much as my impending dismissal.

"Yes, sir," I said timidly. He was out of the room before I had a chance to remind him I had no idea where his office was.

Even though the boss was gone, the rest of the team cleared quickly. Except for Brett, who stayed and helped gather my belongings. Thankfully, he didn't try to chasten me for my outburst.

"Well. Nice knowing you," I said when he handed me my briefcase.

He gave me a sympathetic smile as he walked me to the door. "I'll show you where to go."

But Scott was waiting on the other side of the threshold. "I'll show her there myself, Brett. Thank you."

A familiar look passed between them, one I'd seen before when I'd been out at the club and two men were fighting over who would get my attention. Usually without any regard to who I wanted to give my attention to. Men and their cock fights. It was sweet coming from Brett.

Scott, though, only proved he was the worst of the players. The kind who didn't want the toy for himself but didn't want anyone else playing with it either.

Fuck him.

"Sure thing, boss," Brett said with not-so-veiled animosity.

Not that Scott cared or even noticed. He was striding away before the words were out of Brett's mouth, obviously expecting me to follow.

Stupid me, I did. Like a trained puppy. His footsteps were so quick, I had to hurry to keep up. I didn't even dare throw a last look over my shoulder at Brett, who I was pretty sure watched after us the whole time.

He wasn't the only one. Heads turned as we passed other employees; whispers followed behind me. Either the word had already gotten out about our standoff—not unlikely considering how fast the team had left the conference room—or it just wasn't often that Scott marched women to his office, which was clear at the other end of the hall. A corner spot, of course.

The long walk should have given me time to pull myself together, to come up with an acceptable apology and save my ass. Instead I used the time to validate my anger. After coming on to me at our first meeting, followed by a full whole week of ignoring me, after his complete disregard for my time or my agenda, after his constant scrutinization of my presentations, after he'd patronized me and played on his phone and probably fucked both Eden and Kendra, he was lucky I hadn't made more of a scene than I did.

I wouldn't be as nice when it was just the two of us behind closed doors.

He knew it too. He ushered me into an office the size of my entire apartment, and I could feel the tension between us as I walked past, a thread strung so tight it was bound to break.

And break it did when the doors were closed, and suddenly I found my back pressed against them with Scott caging me in. In shock, I dropped my briefcase to the floor. His face was inches from mine, his blue eyes dark as they pierced into mine before drifting down to my lips.

"This is your fault," he said, and the weight in my stomach dissolved into a hundred butterflies as his mouth crashed over mine. His lips moved hungrily. Tasting me first, then devouring me. As soon as my own lips parted, his tongue licked greedily inside.

And this was why I was doomed.

Because even though I was trapped between his body and solid oak, I was pretty sure he would have let me go if I'd pushed him away.

But I couldn't push him away. I couldn't make my hands do anything but grab onto his lapels and pull him in. I moaned as he deepened the kiss, his palms coming up to my face so he could direct even more than he already was. My hips arched into him. My pussy ached with jealousy. She remembered these lips. She knew what this mouth could do.

My mouth was just discovering, and I was already sure I never wanted to stop.

In the back of my head, a voice of reason shouted the alarm. *What are you doing? You. Must. End. This. Now.*

Sanity returned, and I forced myself to push him away. Sort of.

My hands were still wrapped in his jacket so I was completely aware that I was sending mixed messages. I searched his face trying to understand him. Trying to understand myself. Why did I want him so very, very much?

"We shouldn't be doing this," I whispered, hoping I could urge his resolve to be better than mine.

"Maybe that's why it's so fun." He leaned in again, and I turned my head so his lips met my jaw. It didn't deter him. "You taste so good, Tessa Turani," he said between kisses trailed down my neck. "Everywhere. I can't get enough."

My legs were noodles. He knew just what to say. He knew just how to say it, and I was not strong enough to resist.

But I had to be.

Maybe just one more taste first...

I nudged his face with my chin, bringing his lips back to mine. He brought his body flush with mine. I could feel his erection against my belly, and damn he had a finely shaped cock. I wanted to feel it without clothes between us. I wanted to feel all of him.

Another wave of sense broke over me. "I am not adding charities in place of the ones I'm removing." I could let him take advantage of my body, but not all of me.

He chuckled as he moved his lips along my jaw. "I really, really wish you would."

His facial hair tickled against my skin. His lips found my ear, and now my panties were soaked. If we could just wrap up this stupid deal, then maybe we could explore this. "You know you don't need to see more charities. You don't need to see so much of the ones that are still on the list." My concern likely diminished with the gasp I made as his teeth nibbled on my lobe.

He bucked his hard length against me in response. "Do

that again. Make that noise again. It undoes me."

He lowered his hand from my face, and his next nip at my ear was accompanied by a tweak of my nipple. This time I moaned.

"That's good too. I want all your sounds." He palmed my breast as his mouth once again found mine, and I lost my breath in an attempt to consume him.

"More," I heard myself say, despite the screaming in my brain telling me to stop and think. A thought of reason slipped through my lust-filled daze. I broke off abruptly. "You're purposefully trying to drag this out."

"It's called extended foreplay. The anticipation does wonders for the fucking."

Oh, God. Yes. Foreplay. Fucking. All of that.

Wait, wait, wait. "I meant the presentations. I could tell you which charity to choose, but you're trying to drag it out."

He bent down to press kisses along my décolletage. "Ah. Yeah. Sounds like something I'd do."

"Why?" I wasn't sure anymore if I was talking to him or if I was pleading to God.

Apparently it came across as conversation. Scott pulled back and looked at me pointedly. "Why do you think?"

Because he liked me. Like I liked him. And since he was a spoiled white man with lots of money and privilege, he didn't have to behave like a normal person who would wait until the business was done and then ask me out on a date or a booty call, if that's all he was really interested in.

No, he was the kind of guy who could take what he wanted when he wanted without having to worry about any consequences.

Most of us weren't that lucky.

"Scott…" My eyes fluttered to his lips, but I forced them back to meet his gaze. "You can't do this. You can't hold your power over me like this. It's not fair when you're you, and I'm me."

He stared at me, the war evident inside him. I wonder if he knew how close he was to winning the battle. Once his mouth found mine again, I was certain there'd be no going back.

With a sigh that sounded more like a growl, he pressed his forehead to mine. "I don't understand how I'm the one in power in this situation, Tessa. Because it feels like I'm out of control. It feels like you have all the power over me."

I was putty with a statement like that.

But even dazzled as I was, I recognized he was wrong. "Your feelings are not an accurate measure of reality."

"I'm not sure you have the perspective to determine that." He stood there, his forehead against mine, his hand cupping my neck as we both breathed the same air in and out. In and out. A tilt of my chin, and our lips would meet. I was about to do it. I was weak.

He, on the other hand, was strong. With what seemed like mammoth effort, he separated his body from mine. He took a step back.

Instantly, I missed him. One hand wrapped automatically around myself, the other flew up to cover my mouth, as if to protect it from assault. In actuality, I wanted to touch where he'd been, wanted to hold onto the swollen, used way they felt.

With the space he'd created between us, it was easier to pit rational thought against my feelings of desire. "You can't drag this out," I said, surprising myself with the force of the words. "And you can't kiss me again like this. You can't kiss me again at all."

It broke me to say it. Secretly, I hoped he'd think I didn't mean it. Or that he wouldn't care.

But he was a gentlemanly player. He took another step back. "You're right. I couldn't get through another of those lunches without you knowing where I stand. Next move has to be yours."

And then the charming, seductive man that had been all over me just a moment before disappeared, and the man in charge returned. He straightened his tie and wiped my lipstick from his mouth as he crossed to his desk where he sat down and picked up the receiver of the desk phone. It wasn't until after he'd asked his assistant to get his father on the line that he seemed to notice I was still there.

He shot me a bothered look, and I braced myself for another of his callous remarks. "Tessa, if you stay there one second longer, I don't care if my father's on the other end of this phone, I will have no choice but to go over there and make that pretty pussy mine."

I picked up my briefcase and scurried out. Back in the hall, I had to stifle a giggle. I took a deep breath, but my knees still felt weak. And my lips couldn't seem to stop wanting to smile.

One glare from his assistant, and I pulled myself to-gether. I could not find pleasure in what just happened.

This was my chance to prove myself; I would not lose the opportunity because Scott Sebastian knew how to use his tongue.

I felt more sure as I walked down the hall, my head held high. This was fine. All of it was fine. It might have seemed like a setback, but the ball was in my court. I could resist him just fine.

I almost believed it.

But then I found Brett waiting for me near Eden's desk in the front lobby, and he asked, "How much trouble are you in?" and I knew I wasn't fooling anyone.

"A lot," I answered truthfully.

A whole, whole lot.

TEN

Teyana peered out over the audience below, a little too close to the railing as far as I was concerned. "Kendra has had these box seats all this time and has never bothered to share?"

She hadn't bothered to share this time either. I'd come across the season tickets in a stack of old mail that I'd been sorting through and decided it was insane to let tickets to the Met Opera go to waste.

"She hasn't had them forever. They were a Christmas present from her parents, I think." I knew, rather, according to the message in the envelope I'd found them in. I just didn't know if they'd been a brand-new subscription or a renewal.

Tey gave me one of her and-your-point-is glares. "It's September. How many times do you think she's used them in the past nine months?"

Best-guess estimate? None. "Good point."

I didn't know why I was trying to defend Kendra, anyway. Habit, maybe. Loyalty. But that loyalty was beginning to wane. I was more loyal to Tey, and I could understand her frustration at such an extravagant gift being left unused. Especially one related to the performing arts, something that Tey lived for, despite, as she claimed, not having a creative bone in her body. Her previous full-time job had been managing a program that brought various art forms to inner-city kids. The organization had existed before she came on board, but she'd truly shaped it with her innovation and passion.

Then she got sick.

She still worked for them now, mostly as a consultant and on a very part-time, self-directed basis so she could shift her schedule around when she was having a bad day.

I studied her now as she continued to stare in awe around the theater. Her excitement was evident in her smile, but her eyes looked tired. Just getting from the subway to Lincoln Center when the temperature was above ninety was enough to wear her out on a good day, and I hadn't yet been able to ascertain whether today was one of those good days. She'd likely hide the truth considering how badly she wanted to be here.

"Are you sure you feel up to this?" I asked, hoping the gentle reminder about her health wouldn't piss her off too much.

"Do I feel up to sitting in an air-conditioned theater for three hours? Yes, Tess. I think I can manage. You know I wouldn't miss this performance for the world." She turned away from the railing, leaned her cane against the wall, and sat in the red-upholstered chair at my side. "Besides. I need to hear more about this kiss."

I shook my head with a laugh. Just thinking about the moment with Scott in his office earlier had my pulse picking up. "I've already told you everything. What more could I possibly tell you?"

"He was pressed up against you, right?"

"Yes…" There was some innuendo I was missing.

"Then you need to be telling me details about what the guy is packing. Specifically, length and girth."

"Teyana, oh my God!" I gestured to the box next to us where I'd spotted a handful of old ladies as we'd come in. There were walls between our seats and theirs, but since I could clearly hear their discussion about "Esther's grandson's first term at West Point," it was likely they could also clearly hear us.

"They probably want to know too. They're just not brave enough to ask."

I rolled my eyes. But I went ahead and answered her question—with a lowered voice, of course—because I was as eager to talk about Scott as she was to hear about him. "It felt…significant," I said.

She laughed. "*Significant.*"

"But I really can't make a proper assessment considering I only got to feel it against my belly and not with my hands." The improper assessment I'd made, however, was that Scott Sebastian had much to be proud of.

Tey looked disappointed that I didn't have more intel. "From how heated it sounds like things got, I'm honestly surprised you didn't take the opportunity to explore."

"Hey. You said I absolutely couldn't fool around with him, remember? Now you seem to be encouraging it."

"I said that because it's the smart course of action. It doesn't mean I don't want all the details when you do stupid." She uncapped the water bottle that she'd smuggled in via her oversize bag and took a swig. Staying hydrated was key to managing her symptoms, and I was glad she was taking care of herself.

"You'll always be the first one I tell," I promised. "But there won't be any more stupid. Kissing him was a mistake, and I'm resolved not to let it happen again."

"Mmhmm." She seemed to have as much faith in my commitment as I did, which didn't bode well for my future working relationship with SIC.

As it was, I already couldn't stop thinking about him. Memories of his mouth against mine, of the way his touch had lit up my skin ran in the background the entire afternoon. When I'd chosen the blush slip dress from Kendra's closet, I'd pretended I was choosing it for him. When I'd done my hair up in a messy bun, I'd daydreamed it was so his lips could easily get to my neck. I couldn't get his face out of my mind. Even sitting there waiting for the opera to start, I could swear I saw him in the box across from us.

Wait a minute...

"Teyana, that's him," I whispered, even though he was too far away to hear me. "That's Scott Sebastian."

He was standing and alone, perhaps waiting for someone to join him, and oh my God, was that really him? I squinted to bring him more into focus. It was definitely him, looking hotter than ever in a tux tailored so well he looked sewn in.

Tey sat up, alert. "Where? Over there?" She followed

the nod of my head. I was grateful she didn't point, but then she did something even more embarrassing. She took out her opera glasses and directed them toward him. "Oh, he's as fine as you said he was."

"Tey, stop!" I hurriedly pushed her hand and the glasses down, but it was too late. He'd seen me. His mouth curved into a smirk, and he lifted his palm up to wave.

Instinctually, I waved in return.

Then the lights went down, and the opera's overture began.

Knowing Scott was there changed my entire night. I couldn't concentrate on the performance in the slightest. I felt jittery and restless, and for the life of me I couldn't get comfortable in my chair. I refused to look at him, though I could feel his presence like I was a magnet, and he was true north. I would not give him my attention. I. Would. Not.

Somehow I made it to intermission.

"I need to pee," Tey said, grabbing for her cane.

"And I need a drink. Let's hurry and see if we can beat the lines." Mostly I just wanted to be away from the temptation to glance over at the man who I was beginning to think would be the death of me.

Rush as we did, there was still a long line outside the ladies' restroom when we got there. "Figures," Tey said with a curse. "You don't have to wait with me."

"No, we're staying together." It was the only way I could assure myself that I wouldn't go out seeking the very man I needed to avoid.

Turned out, standing in line for the bathroom was not a

very good place to hide.

"Your man has found us." She nodded with her chin toward the lobby behind us. "Seriously, Tess. He is divine. I can barely look at him, he's so spectacular."

The pull was stronger now, that tug, tug, tug for my attention. Still, I didn't turn around. "Then don't look at him. And he is not my man."

The line moved forward. I took a step sideways so I wouldn't happen to see him in my periphery. I knew if I caught sight of him at all, I'd be a goner. As long as I kept my eyes away, I pretended I had a chance of keeping myself together.

Tey laughed. "Oh my, you have it bad."

"Shut up."

"He can't be here alone, you know. No one goes to the opera alone. Definitely not men like him."

I hated that I'd already been thinking that. "Which is why I'm not giving him the time of day. And you shouldn't either."

"Okay, but he's staring you down like you're a fish he's not gonna throw back. You should go talk to him before he prowls over here." She added the magic words she knew I could never deny. "For me?"

I groaned. Cautiously, I turned so I could take a peek. As soon as my eyes landed on Scott, they were caught. He stood out like an island in a sea of well-dressed men, a champagne flute in his hand. Sexy, refined, and captivating. I could barely move the air through my lungs.

He raised his glass, his grin triumphant, as though he'd won some game I hadn't been aware we'd been playing, except of course I knew what game we were playing, and of course he won because I always lost the stay-away-from-the-hot-guy game.

"Will you be okay?" I asked my friend, my attention still latched on the blue eyes a handful of yards away.

"Yes. Now stop worrying about me and get over there."

I'd known the second I spotted him tonight that going to him would eventually be inevitable. Still, I pretended it had been my choice when I left Teyana and crossed toward him. He watched me take every step, as though I were the only woman in the room. As though he wasn't here for anyone but me.

"I never met you before that party on the roof," he said when I was next to him, "and now you're everywhere."

Since I'd infiltrated his world purposefully, I automatically felt the need to defend myself. "We got the tickets from a friend."

"From Kendra, right? That's the Montgomerys' box."

"Oh. Yes. I forgot you know her." Actively trying to forget, anyway. "I didn't realize you'd be here. Coincidence. Swear to God."

"I wasn't complaining."

The rawness in his tone made my thighs buzz. "Oh."

"Some people say coincidences are meaningful. That it's the universe trying to tell you something."

Serendipity, right. It was pure poetry, the language of the best players, and every single time it made my stomach flutter.

It's all smooth talk, I reminded myself. "You're not one of those people who believes that."

"I don't know. I might be." God, he was good. He didn't even have to talk to be that good. It was in his countenance, in the way his entire body angled toward me. In the way he devoured me with his eyes. "You look... You're breathtaking, Tessa Turani."

My own breath shuddered. "Unfortunately, I feel the same about you."

He laughed, and I was both impressed and irritated that he could see the humor in it. "It is a bit unfortunate, isn't it?"

"A bit." I snagged the champagne from his hand and threw back an unrefined gulp.

My lack of elegance did nothing to dim the intensity of his gaze. "You know what I can't believe?" he asked, taking a step closer, as if we weren't already standing intimately close.

"What?"

"That I let you leave my office today without knowing the color of your panties."

"Scott!" Heat rushed up my face.

"You could end the mystery. Slip them off and give them to me now."

Now heat rushed between my legs as well. The thought of taking my panties off for him, of him realizing how wet he'd made me, of him keeping them as yet another souvenir...

I took another swallow of the champagne and forced myself to remember that our relationship had to be professional only. "You said the next move was mine," I reminded him.

"Is this you making a move?"

"No. And you insinuated that you wouldn't make any more moves unless I did."

"I did insinuate that." His expression grew serious. "I'm going to try real hard to mean it too. Can I start tomorrow?"

I turned my head back toward the bathroom so he wouldn't see my smile. Tey had made headway in the line and was no longer outside where I could see her anymore. Though her support for me had been both angel and devil, I felt a sudden surge of panic without her watching over me. As if the tiny amount of time that she disappeared to pee would be enough for Scott to sweep me into a dark corner and have his filthy way with me.

Was it enough time?

I stopped myself from looking for a dark corner. And wasn't he with someone? "Tey said there's no way you can be here alone."

"Tey? Is that your friend?"

"Yeah." But all I could think about was how it was just my luck that he could do that sexy one-brow-raised thing that made many women weak in the knees. Many women meaning specifically me.

"She's right. I'm not here alone," he admitted, and my stomach dropped. "I'm here with you at the moment."

"I am not with you."

He put both hands on his chest in feigned pain. "My heart."

"Be serious."

"Okay. My blue balls."

I was less successful at hiding this grin. But it wasn't enough to distract me from the question of his unseen companion. My curiosity was stupid, and I said I wasn't doing stupid anymore, but apparently I still was. "Does your date know that you're over here flirting with another woman?"

I was so disappointed in myself, I finished off his champagne.

He put his hands in his pockets, both of them, which made him so sexy my knees went weak, and considered. "I don't think it would surprise her. My mother knows who I am."

"You're here with your mother." It was a bitter relief. Bitter because I hated that it made me relieved at all.

"My father had 'something come up,' and she refuses to go to these things alone. Last minute, of course. He called today and ordered that I take his place. Or convinced me that it was in my best interest to accompany her. I try to ignore those threats as much as possible, but the reality is that he has more influence over me than I'd like to admit."

Out of the corner, I caught Tey coming out of the bathroom, which was my cue to leave, but I also wanted to keep talking to Scott for the rest of the night. Which was another cue that I should leave.

Before I could even attempt a goodbye, he said, "Never thought I'd be so grateful for Dad's mistress."

My full attention was back on him. "Your dad told you to come to the opera with your mother so he could go out with his mistress? He told you that?"

"Not in so many words. But it's a not very well-kept secret. Even my mother knows."

"And she doesn't mind?" I shouldn't have been surprised that the player gene ran in the family, nor that there were many women who endured a wandering husband, but even with how susceptible I was to a man with charm, I knew I'd never stand by a philanderer.

"I don't think it bothers her too much as long as she isn't openly humiliated." To his credit, Scott sounded mournful about the situation.

I was about to say something about how much it must suck to be put in that position, but a sudden commotion outside the bathroom interrupted the thought. As soon as I glanced over and saw a circle of women around a figure lying on the floor, I knew what had happened.

I shoved the empty champagne flute back toward Scott, then ran over to the crowd. "She's with me," I said, pushing my way through. "She's okay. I got this."

Teyana was still passed out, but I knew she'd be embarrassed when she came to, so I tried to break up the scene as much as possible before she did.

"Should we call 911?" someone asked.

"No, she's okay. This happens sometimes."

Happy to be let off the hook, half the crowd dispersed. The other half took off when the lobby lights flashed, indicating intermission was almost over.

I knelt on the ground and bent over Tey. "Hey, are you awake, honey?"

"Does she need some water?"

I looked over my shoulder to see Scott squatting down behind me. The champagne glass had disappeared, and the expression on his face, while calm, said he was eager to help.

I felt unexplainably grateful that he was there. Even though this had happened dozens of times when I was around. Even though I knew exactly how to handle it when it did. It still was nice to not be alone in it for once.

"I got it." I dug in her bag and pulled out the contraband water. "She's always fine once she's on the ground. It's standing that's the worst for her. She should be awake soon." Sure enough, Teyana opened her eyes.

"Tess? Am I on the floor?" She blinked, trying to push away her daze.

I helped her sit up. "You know you are."

She took the water bottle from me and sipped it slowly. I could tell she was feeling better when her focus left me, and she narrowed her eyes in on Scott. "Does he really look that much hotter close up, or am I still in a brain fog?"

"I refuse to incriminate myself with a comment." I could feel him smirking behind me, and I knew I should shoo him away as I'd shooed everyone else. The second act had started, and he was missing it. His mother would likely not be happy about his absence.

Yet I couldn't get myself to do it.

I concentrated on reprimanding Tey instead. "Why didn't you tell me you were feeling POTSie?" It was a term she used for when she was having a bad day, made up from the acronym that described her condition. She rarely fainted out of nowhere. There were usually signs leading up to it, and she'd apparently ignored them.

Tey gave me her guilty look. "Because you would have made me go home."

"I'm making you go home now."

"I know."

"And we're splurging for a cab." I hooked my hand under her shoulder to help her stand up. Instantly, Scott was on her other side, helping as well.

"Scott," he said in introduction. "And you're Tey?"

"Teyana, and I know who you are."

I felt my cheeks burn. He did not need to know that I'd been talking about him. He was already too aware of his effect on me.

He was nice enough not to gloat. "Let me have my driver take you," he offered when we were standing upright.

Instinct told me that the offer was too much, that I shouldn't accept. We'd be fine in a cab.

But with Tey not feeling well, and no idea how long it would take to hail a taxi, refusing didn't seem like an option. "Fine," I grumbled. Then, more gratefully, "Thank you."

While Scott texted for his car, I retrieved Teyana's cane for her. I didn't let her use it walking outside, though. I made her take both my arm and Scott's. If he was going to help, he might as well *really* help.

By the time we made it from the theater to the road, the car was already pulling up. We'd never have been able to get a cab that fast.

Also, it appeared that Scott hadn't been joking about his other car being a Maybach. In a lot of ways, it was more impressive than the limo.

"Holy fuck, this is a car," Tey said as she slid across the

backseat. I started to get in beside her when she stopped me. "You can't just leave without a proper goodbye," she whisper-hissed.

I paused, debating. The car had emergency lights blinking; no one had honked yet. We probably had a minute. "Fine," I mouthed back.

"Take your time." She winked.

I turned back to him, letting the door loosely shut behind me. Now that I was looking at him again, I didn't know what I should say. *Thank you*, obviously. Maybe, *you didn't have to do this. Kiss me*, were the words that seemed to be at the tip of my tongue.

Thankfully, he spoke before I did. "What address should I give the driver?"

Oh, yes. Practicalities.

And now I had to think about this answer. "Uh…"

He gave me that drop-dead sexy eyebrow raise. "Is this a hard question?"

I'd wanted to keep him from knowing who I was before, which meant keeping him from knowing where I lived or where I was staying. Now that he knew I worked for Conscience Connect and the fact that I was sure he'd find out my whole scheme eventually, it seemed less important.

"I'm staying at my boss's," I admitted. "Tey should probably stay the night with me."

"At Kendra's?"

"House-sitting. It's part of the job."

His eyes narrowed in suspicion. "Quite the loyal employee. How close are the two of you?"

I shot back with a suspicious look of my own. "How close are the two of *you*?"

His eye twinkled with the light of a passing car. A beat passed before he answered. "Has she ever mentioned me?"

"Very tangentially." When she'd said the Sebastians were family friends.

"There you go," he said, as if that told me everything.

And maybe it did as far as he was concerned. An employee loyal enough to both run the business pitches and house-sit would surely be an employee who knew the men in her boss's life.

Of course, that wasn't the real situation, but if he thought it was, it probably meant he really hadn't been more than a blip on Kendra's long list of lovers.

I wished that confirmation made me feel better than it did. I would have preferred to discover that he hadn't been on that list at all.

"Well, then," I said, having nothing else to say. Then our eyes locked, and all the earlier restlessness returned. I remembered his lips on me. I remembered the hard shape of his cock pressed against my stomach.

His expression said he was thinking dirty things too. He stepped in closer. "I could come with you."

Could he? "You're here with your mother," I reminded him.

"I could come by later."

The fantasy played out in my head. Tey wouldn't mind if I snuck out. Or if he snuck in. She could have Kendra's bedroom, and we could...

I couldn't be stupid. "I can't." They were the hardest

words I'd ever said. "*We* can't."

"But you want to."

"But I won't."

He let another beat pass. It was hard to think he was wrestling with his desire. I couldn't imagine that he was the kind of guy who ever resisted something that he really wanted.

As though to confirm it, he leaned in, and I was sure he was going to kiss me. Instead, he just opened the door again to help me in. "Just give Rodolpho the address. He'll get you there okay."

Not being kissed left a disappointing ache between my ribs. I wanted to linger. A car honked behind the Maybach.

"Good night, Scott Sebastian," I said reluctantly.

"Good night, Tessa Turani."

I climbed in the car and gave the address to Rodolpho. When the car pulled into traffic, I wondered if Scott watched us drive away. I didn't turn around to look.

ELEVEN

The lunch meetings at SIC had all followed the same pattern. Most of the team arrived before noon, in time to select their drinks from the buffet at the other end of the conference room. Once they were seated, Eden came around with a cart and placed a plate of food in front of each employee, each individualized to their dietary needs—vegetarian, gluten-free, low carb. Scott never arrived until the exact time the meeting was to start, so she'd set a plate at his empty spot, even though he rarely touched any of it.

I'd declined the offer for a meal of my own from day one. It was too hard to present when worrying about food, plus it was easy enough for me to grab something afterward since I didn't have an office to head back to. I'd secretly hoped it would make it easier for me to move the conversations forward with everyone having to interject their comments and questions around mouths full of grilled chicken. That had turned out to be wishful thinking. By Friday, I'd become used to the routine and had resigned myself to accept that it was what it was.

Which was why it was surprising when, at a minute after twelve, Scott still hadn't arrived.

I looked over at Brett as he checked the time on his phone, and I assumed he was noting his boss's tardiness as well. "I guess we should get started," he said. He flipped through the booklet I'd prepared. "Looks like organization number five listed here is for Heart Health. Want to tell us more about it, Tess?"

"Uh." I glanced at the door, expecting to see it open any second now. "You don't want to wait for Scott?"

"Oh, that's right," he said. "You don't work here, so you literally didn't get the memo."

Paris laughed politely. Matt's laugh said he found it genuinely funny.

It was then I realized Eden hadn't put a plate at the head of the table.

"He's not joining us today," Brett went on.

I instantly had feelings about that, though I couldn't quite decide what they were. Confusion? Surprise? Disappointment? A combo of all three with a heavy dose of hurt as well?

I was so busy trying to dissect my emotions, I almost missed the rest of what Brett said. "...that he was confident we were all on the same page, and he no longer needed to be in attendance."

Instantly, I knew it was about me. About the kiss. About my choice to not pursue more of the kissing. Could he not handle the rejection? Had he only shown up to the meetings in the first place because he wanted to get into my pantsuit?

Now I definitely knew what I was feeling, and it was pissed. "I'm so glad that he considers all of this a waste of his time," I said with gritted teeth.

Again, Matt laughed, and I decided that his sense of humor was questionable.

"That wasn't the impression I meant to give," Brett said. "I apologize. Let me rephrase. Scott felt he saw enough from you to realize you know what you're talking about. You've earned his trust."

"Definitely take it as a compliment," Matthew said before stuffing his mouth with a forkful of steak salad.

"Whatever you said to him in his office yesterday must have been quite compelling," Silvia agreed.

"Oh. Huh." My cheeks felt warm remembering that there had been very little saying of anything in his office.

But then I considered what I actually *had* said. That he couldn't drag this out. Had I somehow gotten through to him?

Whether I had or not—whether he'd meant to or not—he'd just simplified my job. He was the one who derailed each meeting with endless questions. Without him in the room, I could get through my pitch in no time.

In fact...

"In that case," I said, mentally shifting my entire agenda, "Forget Heart Health. Forget all the organizations I've already presented. Each of the charities I have listed are worthy and notable, but there is one specific cause that I believe truly fits the needs and wants of SIC more than any other—the Dysautonomia Relief Foundation."

I spent the next twenty-five minutes telling the team in uninterrupted detail about the cause I felt so passionately about. I explained that dysautonomia encompassed several different medical conditions that affected the autonomic nervous system, the system that controls all the "automatic" functions of the body such as blood pressure, digestion, temperature regulation, heart rate, kidney function, and pupil dilation. I told them that people who suffered from dysautonomia had trouble regulating these systems that we take for granted. I described the kinds of things that Teyana battled with on a daily basis—lightheadedness, unstable blood pressure, abnormally high heart rates, fainting—and told them that while some people only had a fainting spell once or twice over their lifetime, many others fainted several times a day, making it difficult to hold jobs or engage socially or participate in recreational activities.

"Dysautonomia is not rare," I said as I neared the end of my spiel. "Over seventy million people worldwide live with some form. There is no cure and treatments are limited, and even though it's a common medical condition, most patients take years to get diagnosed because there is a lack of awareness in both the public and medical profession.

"This lack of awareness is what makes this such a prime candidate for sponsorship. It's a foundation that needs support from a highly profiled corporation. Of course it would be a major coup to have Sebastian Industrial promoting them, but also, it's a major coup for you. It's an original and unique cause but it's also a condition that affects many people, which makes it universal. I know both of those points are important to the team in your selection.

"There's also an opportunity to appeal to those who support the current feminist movement since one form of dysautonomia Postural Orthostatic Tachycardia Syndrome (POTS for short) is primarily a women's disease. It's a disability that health experts compare to the disability seen in COPD or congestive heart failure. The quality of life is likened to that of someone on kidney dialysis. It's estimated to affect one out of one hundred teenagers, and I'm betting that none of you have heard of it. Between one and three million Americans suffer from it, yet because most of these people are women, research and concern has been limited. SIC's promotion of awareness and fundraising for research would be viewed as both on trend and forward thinking. I wholeheartedly believe it's the cause you should be supporting because it will look good for your image, but even more because it's an important cause."

I was out of breath when I'd finished. Not only had I been talking nonstop with no interruptions, but I'd also gotten somewhat passionate in my presentation. More passionate than was probably considered professional. Still less passionate than it deserved.

I refused to regret anything, even when the room was silent for several long seconds.

"Well, wow," Brett said finally, which wasn't exactly comforting.

"That was incredibly eye-opening," Matt said.

"I'm for supporting it." Silvia sounded completely on board. "My niece has that POTS. Her doctors say she could grow out of it, but she's had to quit track, and they are even looking at putting her in a wheelchair."

Paris turned to Matthew. "Didn't that guy in HR have this? Ryan? He had to go on long-term disability because he couldn't make it to work so many mornings."

"Yeah, I remember that," Matthew said. "He fainted at the holiday party and broke his humerus. It was terrible for him. I felt so bad. I'd feel good about choosing this one."

Paris looked thoughtful. "It makes it personal for the corporation. That's a plus. I vote yes."

"I have no problem with it," Matt agreed.

"Seems like it's unanimous then," Brett said.

I couldn't believe it was that easy. "That's it? You all agree to move forward on a partnership with the DRF, so no more pitching other charities? We go on to the coordination meeting from here?"

"That's pretty much it, yes," Brett said. "We'd want to do a thorough background check first, which will take a little bit of time to have ordered and performed. We have a department that handles that, so nothing is needed from you there."

"Okay. Anything else?" It felt like there was a catch. I was waiting for there to be a catch.

Glances were exchanged among the team, something they all knew that I didn't.

"Scott," Paris said.

"Yep. Scott," Matthew echoed.

"We'll have to tell Scott that we settled on an organization," Brett clarified. "He's still the final say."

"But he said he trusted us to make a decision, right? So he'll likely go with whatever the group recommends?"

I was feeling overly confident, maybe because the team had been so enthusiastic. Maybe because I believed Scott wouldn't have left us alone if he didn't truly mean to let us move forward without him.

"He said he trusted *you*." It seemed like a fact Brett wasn't happy about admitting. "In other words…"

Silvia finished for him. "In other words, we back your recommendation one hundred percent. You just have to convince the boss to get on board."

You. Not "we." *I* had to convince him. Me and nobody else.

See? I knew there was a catch.

TWELVE

"**F**ine!" I exclaimed. As if it were actually fine. I swept my things into Kendra's briefcase and stood up. "Totally fine."

Brett stood with me. "You don't have to go right this minute. We still have half the hour left to talk more about it. We can make some recommendations for how to present to Scott. Then make an appointment for later. In fact, worry about all of it next week. His assistant probably isn't even back from her lunch yet."

I knew Brett was attracted to me, which was the reason I assumed he was trying to keep me. He also might have been trying to save me from a confrontation with his "difficult" boss, at least for the day, and I appreciated that. Especially because I knew a meeting with Scott would be difficult on more than one level.

It was a good reason to take Brett up on the suggestion, give myself the weekend to prepare for an encounter with Scott alone. Put together a presentation that solely focused on the DRF. Rehearse my talking points. Make sure I was wearing pretty panties.

No, no, no no no.

My panties could not come into this equation at all. The fact that they'd even crossed my mind was proof that I was not in the least bit ready to see him. That I should sit back down and make a better plan.

Except waiting meant having to be worked into his already busy schedule. It might be days before I could get in, and I didn't want to lose the time I'd saved by cutting out the other charity presentations. And since he'd planned to be at this current meeting once upon a time, there was a chance he was free now.

"Thank you for the offer, but I'm actually fired up from all your enthusiasm. Might as well strike while I'm still hot."

Hot for the project, Tess. Remember that's what you're hot for.

"Okay, then," Brett said, his doubts obvious in his tone. "I wish you luck. We all wish you luck."

The rest of the team echoed his sentiments. And his tone.

I managed to leave with my head held high anyway, though my footsteps did hesitate in the hall when I overheard Matt in the room behind me. "Does it feel like we just sent a lamb to slaughter?"

Their ensuing laughter gave me fuel for the task. I sped up my stride. I'd show them all. I knew what I was talking about. My presentation was solid. Scott was difficult, but he wasn't impossible.

Even if he had hypnotic blue eyes. And charming banter. And irresistible lips.

God, I was so screwed.

Focus on the cause. Teyana and the cause.

As Brett had thought, there was no one at Scott's assistant's desk, but it wasn't an issue since the double doors to his office were wide open. That meant he was definitely inside. From this angle, I couldn't see him, which meant he couldn't see me. Which meant I could still change my mind.

But there was no need to change my mind. We were professionals. This was all good.

I strode through his office with boldness that I hadn't known I'd possessed.

Then came to an abrupt halt when I'd made it halfway into the room. It was farther than I'd made it last time, and while I could tell there was much in my periphery that I would love to examine, my eyes were trapped on him, sitting behind his oversized desk, his leg nonchalantly crossed over the other, ankle to knee, the New York skyline backdropped behind him. He looked like a king on his throne, casually and majestically ruling his world.

"Tessa?" His surprise quickly morphed into a sort of knowing grin. A smoldering smirk that made my stomach flutter and my heart trip. The words I'd prepared were caught in my throat.

I jumped as the doors behind me suddenly closed, pulling my gaze for a fraction of a second. Then it was back on Scott, who'd stood and come around his desk, and even though men who closed their offices doors with a button when a woman walked in were shady as shit, it was also kind of hot, and now my breath caught too because every time I looked at him, he somehow just got more gorgeous, and what had I come in here for again?

"Tessa," he said again, and there was no question in his tone as he stalked toward me. Just raw need that sent an answering jolt to my lower regions. His eyes were dark. His lips were wet.

I wasn't sure if it was me or him who made the official first move. All I knew was that I dropped the briefcase as we came together, our mouths frenzied, our hands frantic, our bodies molded to each other.

"We shouldn't be doing this," I panted in between kisses.

"It's such a very bad idea," he agreed before slipping me his tongue and thereby ending any possibility of talking.

The kissing was explosive, if it could be called kissing. Making out wasn't even an appropriate description of what we were doing. We were desperate and urgent, our bodies moving with singular purpose—a very carnal purpose. With his lips locked on mine, he tore off his jacket, then wrapped his hands in my hair. My hand went lower to stroke the hard outline of his cock, earning me a groan that turned my panties into a flood.

I moaned as well, not only because of the feral sound he'd made, but also because the shape of him in my palm was on the Magnum side of the cock-size scale, and holy mother of all saints, I was definitely going to hell because the only thing I could think about was how fast I could get that magnificent beast inside me.

Scott, thankfully, seemed to have the same agenda. While I worked on his buckle, his hand tugged my skirt up to my waist (thank the Lord I hadn't chosen to wear slacks that morning). I had to abandon the task with the belt half undone when he picked me up, but I didn't complain since it brought my throbbing core to rest against his hard ridge.

His deliciously well-defined hard ridge.

I threw my hands around his neck and hooked my ankles behind him, bucking my hips to get more pressure against my pussy as he carried me...somewhere. I didn't care where. A handful of seconds later, my ass landed on the edge of his desk.

I fell back onto my elbows as he wrapped his fingers into the flimsy material of my panties. "Lift," he ordered, and I did, as eager to have them off as he was. He tossed them aside, then moved to finish undoing his pants. He nodded behind me. "Top drawer on the right. My wallet's there."

This wild with lust and he could still remember protection. It was probably an indicator of just how well rehearsed he was in frantic fucking, but in that moment, he was my hero.

Reaching back, I found the leather wallet, and after very briefly considering going fishing in it myself, I sat up and handed it to him.

"Trade," I said, letting him find the condom while I pushed his pants and boxer briefs down far enough to let his cock spring out.

And wow.

Even after getting a sense of him by touch, I had to

blink. "Mr. Sebastian," I said breathlessly as he rolled on the condom (Magnum indeed). "That is one spectacular cock."

His lips quirked up in a smirk. "I'm glad you approve. Let's see if that pretty pussy of yours agrees."

I already knew she would. Still, I gasped as he drove in, shocked by the feel of his girth inside me. Shocked and very, very pleased. He was enormous, my pussy clamping down on him so tightly that his first few thrusts were stilted and shallow.

Then my body adjusted, and both of us sighed in pleasure as he slid all the way in.

"My pussy agrees," I whimpered. "She really, really agrees."

He flashed a satisfied smile before getting serious about the work of fucking me. And kissing me. And saying dirty, dirty things that made me clench tighter around him.

"I knew it from the minute I tasted it, from the minute I saw it. This was a pussy that needed to be fucked." He hardly sounded out of breath despite the driving tempo of his thrusts.

"Yes, yes," I agreed. "Needed to be fucked." Forget the fact that it shouldn't be fucked. It was too late to pretend I hadn't craved him to the point of distraction.

He rewarded the admission with a searing kiss. "I hope you've given me credit for how much restraint I've shown in pursuing you."

He'd shown restraint?

I wasn't in a position to call him on it. "I think right now we've both demonstrated a lack of self-discipline."

"Does that mean you think we should stop?"

He didn't show any indication that *he* thought we should stop, his fingers digging in at my hips as he tilted me to get a better angle. Still, in case it crossed his mind, I rushed out, "No! Please, no."

He smiled against my lips. "Good because I wasn't going to. But I do like it when you beg."

"Please, please, please," I begged, wanting to make him happy, though I wasn't sure I could take much more. My thighs were quivering with the tension building in my body. I was on the verge of an orgasm that I was half certain would kill me.

"Does my cock feel good, Tessa?"

The way he said my name! "So good. You feel so fucking good."

"Touch yourself. I want to feel you come all over me."

I didn't tell him I was already on the brink. I just did what I was told, putting one finger on the swollen bundle of nerves, letting the rest graze against his cock as he glided in and out of me. I was a powder keg. Being fucked by a man who I desperately wanted, on his desk, in the middle of the day, with all of his employees on the other side of the wall, when I shouldn't be fucking him at all—it was a scenario that lit all my buttons. What had he said last time we'd been in here getting into trouble? *Maybe that's why it's so fun.*

And ohmygod was it fun.

Explosively fun. Even knowing it was coming, my climax caught me off guard as it burst through me. Stars pressed against my closed lids. My muscles went rigid as they convulsed with pleasure. I let out a cry that Scott had to stifle with a hand clamped over my mouth.

"Fuck, yes. That's a good girl." He looked down between us, watching as he forced his cock into my clenching pussy. "God, you're so wet. So tight. So fucking perfect."

His words broke off into a grunt, his body jerking as he hit his own climax. Still not recovered myself, I forced my eyes open so I could watch him lose control. It did something to me to see him like that. As majestic as he looked when he was composed and in charge, he was just as striking when he'd come undone, and for the briefest of moments, I wished I could see that version of him over and over and over.

But who was I kidding? This would be a one-time thing. He was the type who didn't like repeat pussy. I knew that going in.

I was still looking at him when he opened his eyes. Too late, I turned my head away, but he put a hand to my cheek and brought it back. His lips pressed against mine, softly, a sharp contrast to the frenzy from moments before.

"This isn't where I thought I'd first fuck you," he said.

My heart skipped, fool that she was, wanting to find meaning in his words.

My head knew better. Thank God she was the one in charge of my mouth. "Is that a line you use often?"

He brushed his thumb against my skin, his expression serious. "I mean it. I think about it. Think about fucking you. A lot. In detail."

There was a possibility for hope in that statement. What was the point in saying it *after* he'd gotten in my panties unless he wanted to get in my panties again? Maybe this didn't have to be a one-time thing. Maybe I *could* see that look over and over and over.

It was easier thinking that it wasn't an option. Because when it *was* an option, when I was the one who got to say yea or nay, I would undoubtedly say yea, and I knew exactly what that would lead to—lots of amazing sex and a big fat broken heart. Mine, to be specific. Been there, done that; I was wise enough to know better.

Knowing better meant believing the option was not on the plate. "And now it should be out of your system." I pushed him away, then snatched a handful of tissues from the box on his desk so I could clean myself up.

"Come on, Tessa." He took the crumpled-up tissues from me, grabbed another to wrap the condom in, then threw all of it in the garbage by the side of his desk. "Are you really going to be like that?"

"Like what?"

His desk phone buzzed before he could respond. Reaching around me, he pushed the intercom, simultaneously giving me a glare that told me to be quiet. "Yes, Sadie?"

Of course his assistant had a sexy name. She was probably blonde and five foot nine with big boobs. Oh, and they'd probably fucked plenty of times. I hadn't forgotten that I'd met him finger-banging the front office receptionist.

"Your father called down to let you know he's on his way down for your one o'clock meeting."

Scott's expression changed instantly. He checked his

watch as though to confirm the time, then quickly began to do up his pants. "Thanks for the reminder," he told her, then hung up before she could say anything. "Hate to cut this short, but that's our cue to wrap this up."

I pulled myself together while he went into full-on clean-up mode, picking up my discarded panties, then his jacket, then retrieving my abandoned briefcase. I met him in the middle of the room where he handed me the latter. He put on the jacket, and not surprisingly, stuffed my panties in the inside pocket. "These, I keep."

"Yeah, yeah, I know the drill." That there was a drill, that I was being ushered out in a rush, were both reminders that this absolutely could not happen again.

At the door, with my hand on the handle, he stopped me with a hand clasped possessively around my neck. "This discussion is to be continued," he said before kissing me once more.

A spine-tingling kiss that made it obvious to me that whatever I wanted to believe about how Scott Sebastian felt about me, he most definitely wasn't out of my system.

I was still dazed when he pulled away. Without a word, he fixed my lipstick and opened the door. "I'll look over those materials and talk to you more next week, Ms. Turani," he said a little louder than he needed to. "Thanks for stopping by."

God, he was good. So experienced with daytime trysts that he could shift gears in an instant.

I made every effort to do the same. "That's. Yes. Same. Thank you."

Obviously, I didn't quite pull it off as well as he had.

But I did manage to walk out without falling flat on my face, an amazing feat considering how much my knees were knocking.

As I passed Sadie's desk on my right—oh, she was a sultry redhead; figured—a distinguished man with salt and pepper hair and blue eyes matching Scott's passed me on the left.

He glared as I walked by, or that might have been my imagination, or maybe the scowl was for his son who I heard greet him behind me. "Surprised to see you down here, Dad. I'd assumed our meeting would be in your office."

"I prefer to keep you on your toes."

Then the doors closed, or they were simply out of earshot. I didn't bother to look back and check. It took all my concentration just to put one foot in front of the other and get myself the hell out of there.

I'd made it to the main reception area before someone tried to stop me. "How'd it go?" Silvia asked.

"Good, good." I kept walking, eager to be on my way. "Late. Gotta—" I pointed in the direction I was going.

"That's great!" she called after me. "Congratulations!"

It wasn't until I was in the elevator and the doors were shut that I realized what she was congratulating me for.

Shit! The foundation!

THIRTEEN

Fortunately, I was able to get an appointment with Scott for eleven-fifteen on Monday.

"He'd like to know if this is business or...?" Sadie, the busty redhead, had asked when I'd called.

"Business," I'd said a little too quickly. "Definitely, definitely business." I wasn't sure who needed to know that more—me or Scott? Both of us had proven our will-power wasn't exactly the best.

Sadie had confirmed the meeting and even sent an email invitation, making it all official. With that set up, my mind was free to ruminate on other things. Specifically, what had happened in Scott's office. How good it had felt. How wrong it had been. How the wrong of it had contributed to the feeling good.

By the time I'd fallen asleep, I'd replayed the scene a hundred times. Thank God for the portable purse vibrator that Tey had gotten me for my last birthday because my hands weren't doing it. Though, knowing Kendra and her spending habits, she probably had several still in their boxes hidden somewhere if I decided I wanted to explore.

The next morning, I woke up to a text from Brett.

> I'm going to this today. Want to join me?

The link that followed took me to an informational seminar at the Jefferson Market Library hosted by the Dysautonomia Relief Foundation.

I closed my eyes without responding, phone still in my hand and a smile on my face. It might have been good business for him to seek out more information on his own, but I had a feeling his interests were more about spending time with me. Which was sweet. He was definitely a man who would be on my radar if we weren't working together.

And if my radar wasn't completely monopolized with Scott.

I groaned remembering. Maybe it was more of a moan. A groan-moan, one that I repeated when I stretched and felt the reminder of yesterday's activities between my legs.

As bad of an idea as it was, staying in bed and thinking about it all day long sounded like a good agenda. I already knew plenty about the DRF. I didn't need a seminar. Besides, I didn't want to send the wrong message to Brett by accepting the invitation.

I forced myself to sit up and type out a reply. Halfway through the message, I had second thoughts. What if Brett talked to the presenters? What if he mentioned me? What if he mentioned the possible sponsorship?

While it was most likely that whoever was sent to speak wouldn't know anything about Conscience Connect or the contract, there was still a chance that they did. A chance that they knew the contract was with Kendra. A chance they knew that Tess Turani was merely her assistant.

I flicked back to the link to check the time of the seminar before shooting a reply to Brett.

Meet you there.

Then I jumped out of bed and hopped in the shower. I had a little over an hour to get ready and make it to the Flatiron District. If I was going to be on time, I had to move at warp speed.

"I don't think I learned a single thing today that you hadn't already gone over yesterday," Brett said as we walked out of the library three hours later.

"That's not true," I laughed. He was being polite. The seminar had been quite thorough, including talks from two patients who suffered from different forms of dysautonomia.

Turned out I needn't have worried about the presenters. Not only were they volunteers who probably had no clue about the foundation seeking sponsorship, Brett also had no interest in speaking to them.

Of course he may have if I wasn't with him. Or he might not have gone to the seminar at all, and even if he felt like he hadn't walked away with any new information, Brett seemed to be more devoted to the cause now. Either way, it wasn't a wasted trip on my part.

"Okay, I did learn one thing." He stopped walking and turned to me. "I learned that you are very expressive when you're listening to someone speak about something you care about."

My face went warm. I'd been told that before, told that I'd often animate along with the speaker. It was completely unconscious on my part, and I struggled not to be embarrassed by it.

"Was I completely distracting?"

He gave me a smile that told me the distraction had been welcome. "I'm sure no one noticed but me. And possibly that grumpy man sitting behind us."

"He *was* grumpy, wasn't he? I could feel his frown even when I wasn't looking at him."

We laughed about it and about whatever Brett said in reply, which I missed because a sudden unbidden memory of Scott flashed in my head, stealing my attention, so I just chuckled when Brett did as if I'd heard the joke.

How dumb was I to be fantasizing about the hot player who probably hadn't thought twice about me since I'd left his office when a perfectly nice, handsome, sweet man was standing right in front of me? A man who was clearly interested.

When our laughter faded away, his gaze remained. "I don't know about you, but listening to people talk about medical conditions seems to have worked up an appetite."

A decent woman would have kindly declined. He was too good of a person to lead on.

But I was still thinking inappropriate thoughts about a

man that I had no business thinking about, and a quick bite with Brett might be just the opportunity to discover more about his cousin.

I scanned our surroundings and spotted a street vendor. "I wouldn't mind grabbing a hot dog. Nice enough day; we can sit out here and eat it on the library grounds."

His expression was mixed, as though he was glad for more time with me but disappointed that I hadn't suggested something sit-down. Whether he took it as a sign that I wasn't into him or that I was committed to maintaining a professional relationship for the time being, I didn't know.

Either way, he seemed to realize he should take what he got. "Sounds perfect to me."

Half an hour later, we'd each polished off a full-length chili dog and shared a chocolate chip cookie. Brett was still working on a bag of chips while I nursed a bottled iced tea, and though we'd chatted about everything from SyFi's *The Expanse* to the best kinds of dogs to have as pets, I hadn't yet found a way to bring up what I really wanted to know.

Then, he did it for me. "Silvia said you got Scott on board."

My stomach tightened. This was not quite the way I'd hoped he'd come up. I was doing my best not to think about the predicament I'd gotten myself in when I'd chosen to bang the VP instead of presenting him with the team's decision.

Still, I couldn't hide from the facts.

I took another swig of my drink while I considered my response. I didn't want to lie to Brett. But my whole relationship with SIC was a lie, so it was kind of too late for that now.

"There's still a little bit I need to iron out with him." Downplayed, but honest. "I have a meeting with him on Monday before our lunch."

Now I just had to hope that Brett wouldn't bring it up to Scott before I had the chance.

"That's great. On the one hand, I'm surprised that you were able to sell him so quickly. On the other, it's hard not to buy when you're the one selling."

I looked away so he wouldn't see my eye roll. That was a player line if I'd ever heard one. Maybe I didn't give Brett enough credit.

Once that thought had passed, I worried about what he'd said for a different reason. "I hope you aren't suggesting that he'd only sign on because...well." I wasn't sure how to frame it.

"Because you're a beautiful woman? I have no doubt that Scott is influenced by pretty ladies, but I'm also positive that he would never sign onto something that he didn't believe in. I didn't mean to imply anything except that you know what you're doing. And Scott needs to get this sponsorship rolling. He's getting pressure from the big guy. As you probably already know, the company is involved right now in some legal battles about one of the pipelines, and Henry is hoping that launching the support of a foundation will divert public attention."

It was the way with a lot of the companies that Kendra matched with charitable organizations. Sometimes when she got wind of bad PR, that was exactly when she'd swoop in and introduce the idea of sponsorship.

Not for the first time, I wondered why it was that she hadn't hit up SIC herself.

But I was more curious about other things. "Henry. That's Scott's dad?"

"Right. He's the executive chairman. Co-chairman, technically. With his brother." Brett paused to study me. "Your expression says you still haven't googled who's who at SIC."

"That's not true. I did. I just didn't google who's who in the Sebastian family." The only reason I'd been able to resist was because I knew a thorough search would have delivered images of all the women Scott had ever been photographed with. I was already struggling with confidence. I didn't need to obsess about supermodels and elite royalty and whomever else he undoubtedly had dated/hung out with/banged.

"Well, then let me give you a lesson." Brett gathered our trash and cleared a space on the ground between us. Then, using a plastic fork, he drew a mark in the dirt. "Irving Sebastian founded Sebastian Industrial Corp when he was a wee lad. He's ninety-five now, so it was a long time ago. Built the whole empire from scratch. Made lots and lots of money, obviously. Kept the stock private, and his wife is dead, so it's mostly divided among his children."

Brett drew five lines below the first. "Henry is the oldest. Then Reynard, Samuel, August, and Arthur. Henry and Reynard run SIC together. Arthur is on the board. Samuel and August moved over to Sebastian News Corp when the company split in the nineties."

"All his children were boys?"

"Didn't you know? Irving Sebastian was so rich, he could even influence genetics." He was joking, but I could hear the hint of bitterness. "In all seriousness, the abundance of boys is creepy. It continued to the next branch of the family tree. Henry, for example." He drew five more lines below one of the lines on the level above. "Besides Scott, he has Miles, Cole, and Zach. They stopped when they had Sydney. She gets doted on."

Four older brothers? "Yeah. I can imagine."

Brett went on to fill in all the branches on the tree, explaining who did what and who should be avoided (both Reynard's sons) and who he liked (August's line). About half of all the descendants had some sort of job with SIC or the News Corp.

"I almost ended up at the News Corp myself," he said at one point. "Because I'd much rather work for Samuel and August, but I just wasn't interested in the work. I don't have to deal with Henry or Reynard personally anyway. And Scott can be hardheaded, but he's really not that bad."

Scott and the term *hardheaded* threatened to take my mind places it shouldn't go. I shook off the dirty thoughts and thought instead about the severe-looking man who'd passed me as I'd left Scott's office. "I saw Henry yesterday. Briefly. He did seem formidable, even at a glance."

Brett shrugged. "He's the man in charge of it all. I suppose that's what it takes to work in that position. I sure wouldn't want that pressure. I definitely wouldn't want to be one of his sons."

I looked over the family tree he'd diagrammed in the

dirt and frowned. "Wait. Where do you fit into all of this?"

"Ah, yes. The Lessers." He drew another line next to Irving at the top. "My grandma is Ida, Irving's little sister. She got pregnant out of wedlock, total embarrassment in those days. But Irving was protective and family-oriented, so he made sure to take care of her and kept the scandal hush-hush. She kept the Sebastian name. All that stirred lots of rumors, naturally. People saying that Irving was the father." Brett shuddered at the idea. "It's a fun piece of gossip, but not true. I think Grandma actually got knocked up by a grifter, though that's never been confirmed.

"Anyway, she had twins, Luke and Luis. Luke is my dad." He drew more lines on the tree. "All of us over here are The Lessers. We're well off. Irving made sure both my dad and my uncle have jobs. We'll get an inheritance when Irving dies. Nothing like what the Greater Sebastians live with."

He put up a hand as if to emphasize his next point. "I'm not complaining. At all. It's easy to get seduced by all that the Greaters have in terms of luxury, but I've seen first-hand what all that money can do to people. They're too hardened. Too spoiled. Too difficult to get close to. They exist in their own world, and even when you think you've been invited in, you never really are."

He didn't mean it as a warning, but I knew if I were smart, I'd take it as one.

So why was I intrigued with Scott Sebastian more now than ever?

I'd just curled up on Kendra's sofa, remote in hand, when my phone rang. It was Saturday night, so of course I wasn't surprised to see the caller ID say RESTRICTED. Leave it to Kendra to have no regard for personal time.

I forced a smile before I answered, knowing she'd hear it in my voice. "Hey."

Except it wasn't Kendra who responded. "You were with Brett."

"What?" I'd heard what he said. I was just fl abbergasted about having Scott Sebastian on the other end of my phone.

"I know you heard what I said." His voice rumbled, a bit like he was scolding me. A bit like he was sharing a secret.

My skin sprouted goosebumps in response.

And because oh-my-freaking-god Scott Sebastian had called me. Which meant he was thinking about me. Like I was thinking about him.

Maybe not that much. I was thinking about him at an awful embarrassing level. He'd probably just had a fleeting thought about me, and on a whim, the way bored spoiled rich boys do, he searched out my phone number on a Sat-urday night and called me.

Yeah, even if he wasn't thinking about me at embar-rassing levels, it was enough to be meaningful.

I had to play this cool. "Hello to you, too, Scott."

"Hello, Tessa." Oh, the things it did to me when he said my name. "Tell me why you spent today with Brett."

Scott had a power over me, one that I hated admitting to, but real nonetheless. He gave me a command, my body wanted to obey it. It was why I'd already lost two pairs of panties to the man.

I was also a fool. A practiced one. Ready to pounce on any hint that I might have power over him as well. "How do you know how I spent the day? Were you spying on me?"

"I have my ways."

"Okay, well. You can use your ways to find the answer." I'd been going for casual indifference, and I must have passed it off, because he gave me what I wanted.

"Brett mentioned it tonight at this family thing. Someone's birthday. Don't ask who. I didn't pay attention. Point is, there were too many nosy people around to probe him for more information, so I'm coming to you to get the answer."

It was the perfect opportunity to tell him about the DRF. Explain the foundation, get him on board. At least I could warm up the conversation for Monday.

But my thighs still ached from wrapping around him the day before. My skin was tingling, my heart was pounding, and given the choice of talking business or flirting, I was very much interested in the latter.

"Why do you care?" I wanted to sound nonchalant, but I had a feeling it came across as eager.

"I think you know why."

"I don't think I do."

A beat passed, and I worried I'd fucked up somehow. When he spoke again, his tone was more demanding. "Do

I need to be concerned?"

"About Brett coming on to me?" I wanted him to be jealous about Brett, but I couldn't believe he really was. Jealous over a Lesser? Over *me*?

Scott made a sound of annoyance. "You forget that I know Brett. He is too professional to make a move on a woman he's doing business with."

Either Scott was doubting what he knew, or he…

I suddenly saw this from his angle. He'd seen me get excited when I'd met "a Sebastian" at that party. He'd witnessed my lack of professionalism when I'd let him kiss me. When I'd fucked him in his office. Now he'd learned I'd spent the day with Brett. Why wouldn't he think I'd be like that with this man too?

Even understanding, I was offended. And hurt. "So the person you're potentially concerned with is me."

"I know you *want* to stay on the right side of the ethics line…"

I gritted my teeth so I wouldn't say something equally as shitty. "That is a problem I only seem to have with you."

"That's all I needed to know."

"And you don't need to worry about it being a problem in the future," I added, his triumphant tone only adding fuel to my annoyance. Fuck him. Fuck me too for thinking there might be something between us, but mostly fuck him.

But then his voice fell low and serious. "It's not out of my system, Tessa."

"What's not?"

"You. Not anywhere near."

Whoa.

I had to work to keep breathing.

"Tell me you feel the same." He was insistent. The natural urge to tell him whatever he wanted to hear bubbled up inside of me.

Despite the urge, it was because it was the truth that I answered how I did. "I feel the same."

"Good. We're getting somewhere."

I couldn't begin to imagine where it was getting us.

Strike that. I could imagine it too well. I was very good at imagining scenarios of happily ever after with men like Scott Sebastian. Men who very much only wanted happily for the moment. Ten times out of ten, those kinds of fantasies got my heart broken.

I could not let myself imagine anything with Scott.

My self-warnings were interrupted by voices in his background.

"Where are you?" I asked.

"Still at the family thing."

It definitely sounded like it could be a party. But there was one voice that was closer than the others. "Come on, Scott," she said.

She. A familiar she. And it didn't belong to anyone in the family, though she'd been at the last family party the Sebastians had thrown. "Is that *Eden*?"

The background noises grew muffled, as though he'd turned away for privacy. "Are you jealous?"

"No. I'm curious."

"And jealous. You don't have to hide that from me, Tessa. I like it."

His gloating should have been a turnoff, but of course it wasn't. It made me feel all dizzy and breathless and wanted, which was extra stupid considering he was with fucking Eden. "Why is Eden with you?"

"Now you see how I felt. Not fun, is it?" He was enjoying this way too much.

"See, but you forget that I've witnessed firsthand what kind of relationship you have with Eden." I couldn't believe I was giving him this much. Allowing myself to be this vulnerable.

"Brett brought her," he said, taking pity on me. "They're old friends. And no, I'm not going to touch her tonight, even if she begs. *When* she begs. Does that make you feel better?"

"I don't know how it makes me feel," I lied because there was no way I was admitting just how much better it made me feel.

He chuckled. "Keep telling yourself that, Tessa. It's not ever going to make it true." Eden's voice sounded in the background again. More urgent. More annoyed. "It seems the cake thing is happening. I have to go."

"Oh. Okay." It was too soon. I wasn't ready to hang up. I wanted to keep flirting and baring myself and hating myself for letting myself be so exposed. None of which I could say. I stuttered looking for something that I could. "I'll...I'll..."

Fuck. I'll...what?

Scott stepped in for me. "I know. I'll be thinking about you too."

For a long time after he hung up, I clutched my phone

to my chest and grinned.

FOURTEEN

"I've been thinking about your problem," Teyana said on Monday when she called. "And I think I know what you need to do."

I had a semi-good idea what she was referring to as my problem. I'd spent the previous day with her, and pretty much all I'd talked about was Scott. How confusing he was, how much I still wanted him, how worried I was that I was going to fuck the DRF over because of my silly obsession.

I was eager to accept any help she could give.

I pulled my phone away to check the time. Fifteen minutes until I had to leave for the Sebastian Center. I'd have to multitask. After turning on the speaker, I set my cell on the bathroom counter and went back to applying my mascara. "Give it to me."

"So. You want to keep this deal with the DRF on the level. I get that. But let's be honest here. You're already there under false pretenses. You've already banged the guy in charge. You've already crossed the ethics line. There's a better chance than not that you'll end up messing around with him again the minute you're alone with him today."

"That's a fairly accurate summary of the circumstances." And explained my current state of self-loathing. "Is this supposed to be helpful?"

"Extremely. Hear me out."

"Still listening." I blinked a couple of times and studied myself in the mirror, making sure my eye makeup looked even.

"Instead of fighting the attraction, you use it."

With a frown, I stared down at my phone. She couldn't mean what I thought she meant. "Are you suggesting that I pimp myself out in order to get this contract signed?"

"I wasn't going to be that crass, but…"

I switched off speaker mode and put the phone back to my ear. "I am not going to offer sex in exchange for this, Teyana. Not only is that demoralizing and anti-feminist, it's also completely unethical—"

"Already crossed that line, remember?"

I ignored her interruption. "And if anyone found out that's what I'd done, any progress I made would be null and void. Why would I do that to the DRF? Why would you want me to risk that?"

"Calm your tits, Tess. I'm not saying you exchange sex for anything. Just, don't fight against the desire. Lean into it. We both know Kendra certainly does. She's probably slept with half of the men she's sold to, and everything has worked out fine. So Scott wants to fool around more, right? Go in, flirt a bit, then tell him the clothes stay on until you get the business out of the way. You'll both be motivated to the task if there's a reward at the end, a reward that is going to happen regardless of any contract being signed. A reward you've already received."

I opened my mouth to argue more, then closed it again when I realized it was a lost battle. I truly wanted to keep to the moral high ground, but I'd already wandered off that path so long ago, I could barely see it in the distance. Would I be able to have a conversation with him that didn't end with our mouths locked? Past experience said that it would take both of our resolve if I wanted to even give my pitch before we fell into each other's arms.

The more I thought about it, the more Teyana's suggestion seemed like the only way to go, whether I liked it or not.

With a sigh, I looked down at the pantsuit I was wearing, chosen specifically because it would be hard to get out of. "In that case, I'd better change into something less restrictive."

An hour later, wearing a flowy skirt and no panties, I checked in with Sadie outside Scott's office. "I have an eleven-fifteen appointment. Tessa Turani."

I winced as soon as I said it. Now I was referring to myself as Tessa? What was this man doing to me?

The woman hadn't bothered to look up from her computer screen until I'd given my name. Now, she scanned me up and down, her mouth tight while she appraised me.

"He said to send you on in when you arrived," she said with a hint of curiosity.

"Uh, okay." I failed to see why it was such an odd request.

"He never does that," she explained. "He's a 'buzz me when they arrive' type of guy. Makes me think you must be special."

It was tempting to believe that. It was my favorite fantasy—pretending that the current player I was attracted to thought I was more than just a notch in his bedpost. Tey referred to it as my romance-colored glasses, saying that I always saw love in what was very clearly lust.

Knowing this about myself didn't stop my yearnings, but it did make it easier for me to separate fact from fiction. The fact here was that I was most definitely not special to Scott Sebastian.

"He just knows we're on a deadline," I assured Sadie, though to be honest, I wasn't sure why Scott had given her that direction, especially when I'd made it clear when I'd made the appointment that this was to be a business meeting.

Actually, I did know why. Because he knew as well as I did how well we did business together. Because he was eager to fool around.

All the more reason that Tey's plan of approach had been the best. Now I just had to figure out how to put it into action. Standing here looking like a fool while I stared down his office doors wasn't getting me anywhere.

"I'll, uh, go on in then," I said to Sadie.

"Yes. I think you should do that."

With a burst of courage, I pushed into his office.

He was on the sofa, listening intently to someone on the phone, but he looked up and nodded when he saw me. Quietly, I closed the door behind me and set my briefcase down next to it after taking out the expanded booklet I'd made for the DRF from the outer pocket. Then, when he gestured for me to come closer, I crossed the room to him.

Yep. That's all it took. A little crook of his finger, and I was on my way.

God help me.

When I actually made it over and sat down across from him, I realized I was doing better than I'd thought. This wasn't going to be as hard as I'd imagined. He was breathtaking (as always) and stupid sexy as he typed something into his laptop and spouted off something in Spanish to the person on the phone, but there was a coffee table between us, and the air of professionalism cloaked the room.

Was it possible I didn't need to use my wiles after all?

Then Scott finished his call, set his laptop aside, and pinned his attention on me, and with his blue eyes boring into me with that devilish glint, I was undone.

"Tessa." His voice was heated. "I've been told this meeting is, much to my dismay, of a business nature, and so I've promised myself I'll be on my best behavior. But you should know—my best behavior is still pretty bad."

I was pretty sure I purred.

So back to Tey's plan. Sort of. "Good thing, then, that I'm here to try to manipulate you with sex."

His mouth curled up into a wicked half-grin. "I'm intrigued. What exactly are you after?"

Ugh, this felt wrong. In a bad way.

But there was no going back now. I handed him the booklet. "I presented the team with the organization that I am convinced is the best choice for SIC sponsorship. Everyone unanimously agreed. It's outlined here in detail for you to look over, which I hope you do, but I'm also hoping that you will green light it immediately, so we can go onto the next phase. I know we're both eager to get this deal moving along, and if you approve the coordination meeting right now, well. Then we still have forty minutes before the team meeting to, uh, play."

It was official. I was not very good at using sex as a weapon.

That thought was confirmed when he didn't react at all to my proposal, his expression instead growing serious as he opened the booklet and began skimming the material. "Dysautonomia," he said after a few seconds. "Is that what Teyana has?"

I hadn't expected him to be that astute, or for him to even think about a woman who he'd met for a handful of minutes. "Um. Yeah. It is."

"I thought it might be when I read through the previous materials you provided." He shut the booklet. "All right. It's approved."

It couldn't be that easy.

I narrowed my eyes. "You're that eager to get to the, um, playing, that you're really just going to say yes without thoroughly thinking it through?"

"I am eager, but I'm not saying yes without thinking it through. I've read the materials you have given us. I've done some extra research on my own. The DRF was the one I was leaning toward myself. You say it's the best one for us, I trust you. I'm glad the team has come to the same conclusion."

"But you've been super thorough. You made me go through all those meetings discussing organizations you weren't interested in, asking a million questions."

"And you already called me on that. I was dragging it out, and now I'm not." He leaned back against the leather sofa and crossed one ankle over his other knee.

He looked laid back and in charge because he was. He didn't see how he demonstrated his power, but that's what all this had been—a big power trip. All of this could have been decided in one meeting. He'd turned it into five. Six if we counted this one. And I did. It was frustrating enough to make me pissed. And I would be.

If it weren't for the fact that he'd clearly done all the power playing because he was attracted to me.

And, damn, if I weren't a sucker for that shit.

I also really, really cared about this sponsorship. "You mean it? I can tell the team today that we're moving forward, and I can schedule a coordination meeting?"

"I mean it." He picked up his laptop. "I'll order the background check right now. It should be back by Wednesday. You can schedule a meeting as early as Thursday. I'll make sure Sadie knows to work around whatever time you give her."

That wasn't going to help to discredit her notion that I was special, but what did I care?

Right now I was actually feeling pretty special. I was

this much closer to getting what I wanted, and it was because of Scott. I couldn't help being grateful, power games or not. "Thank you. Truly. I wasn't expecting you to be won over so easily. I'm...thank you."

"You're welcome. Thank you for bringing the DRF to Sebastian Industrial." He finished ordering the background check, closed the laptop, and set it on the coffee table. "Now we can discuss sex *without* manipulation."

I felt all sorts of ridiculous for thinking I would have been able to manipulate the man into anything. But that didn't do anything to diminish the want I had for him. It was a light switch. All he had to do was be in the room, and I was aroused.

So if he was going to offer… "Okay."

His eyes sparked with excitement. "Okay, what? We can discuss it?"

"I don't think we need to *discuss* it."

He rubbed his chin with one long finger, a smile toying with his lips. "Say it. Say what you want."

I could feel my cheeks flush. "Really?"

"If you can't say it, how am I supposed to know what *it* is?"

Oh, yes. I'd forgotten he was the kind of guy who liked to hear it out loud. Especially after the way I'd tripped over offering sex earlier, of course he was going to make me say it.

I took a breath for boldness. "I want you to fuck me."

The smile landed for real. "I'm so glad that's what you want, Tessa. Because that's exactly what I want, too. You mentioned that we'd 'play,' and that gave me an idea. Can we...make it a game?"

Curiosity outweighed any hesitancy. "What kind of game?"

"I was thinking we'd play 'Tessa earns the coordination meeting green light.'"

"*Earn* it?"

"You know what I'm saying. Decide if you want to play—I'll fuck you no matter what, so don't let that pressure you. I've greenlit the DRF for the next phase, no matter what." His gaze turned dark, his voice dropped low. "But let's pretend it isn't. Pretend you have to—what were the words you used?—*manipulate* me in order to get it."

Oh, God. This was wrong. The good kind of wrong this time, and I was there for it. "Does it make me a terrible person that I find this scenario you're suggesting really fucking hot?"

"It makes you a goddess. I knew you were kinky. The minute I realized you watched on the rooftop."

I wasn't about to tell him that my kinky side had only come out since meeting him. He didn't need any more of a head trip. Regardless, I was on board.

Before I crawled onto his lap, though, I needed one more confirmation. "This really has absolutely no effect on the DRF? If I walk out right now, you're still willing to move them to the next vetting stage?"

No way was I walking out. I'd caught sight of the bulge in his pants, and my mouth was already watering. His cock would be mine.

"Swear on my Grandma Adeline's grave. Do you want me to put it in writing?"

He'd ordered the background check. That was good enough.

Emboldened by the need tugging inside me, I crawled onto the coffee table between us, giving him a front-row view of my cleavage. "Mr. Sebastian," I said, seductively lilting my voice. "I know this isn't very professional, but I'm desperate. I really want SIC to sponsor the Dysautonomia Relief Foundation. It means more to me than I can even express, and I would do anything to get it. Anything. Can you tell me how I can earn it?"

I swear the bulge got bigger. Yes, I was watching.

He pretended to ponder. Casually. As if he didn't have a noticeably raging hard-on. "I might be willing to consider it. What exactly did you have in mind, Ms. Turani?"

I nodded toward his crotch and blinked innocently. "I could help you take care of that."

"Could help me with what?" Always wanting to hear the filthy words.

I knew better. I tried again. "I could suck your cock, Mr. Sebastian."

"I suppose that might be interesting." He spread his legs apart, inviting me to kneel in front of him.

I scrambled down to the floor at a speed that couldn't have been sexy. It didn't matter. His cock was as hard as any steel Sebastian Industrial produced. I could see the clear outline. I could feel it as my hands brushed against it while I rushed to undo his pants.

It felt like it took forever before I had the zipper down and his cock out. Finally, there it was, big and bloated, the crown an angry red. I'd never realized how satisfying the right cock could be just to look at. I could have stared at it all day. Could have leisurely run my hands up and down the hot column of flesh and been content.

But that wouldn't "earn" me anything. And I really did want to have it in my mouth.

Sucking in my cheeks and flattening my tongue, I drew his head past my lips and was rewarded with a moan. That was all the encouragement I needed to take him in farther, as far as I could and still be comfortable. Then I pulled off of him and repeated the motion, again and again. Slow enough to be able to savor his taste and his scent. Slow enough to taunt him.

Scott made pleased sounds as I worked. Frustrated sounds too when he clearly wanted a different speed than I'd set. I planned to get there, eventually, but before I could, he wrapped his hand tightly in my hair so that my head couldn't move.

"Another way you could earn your sponsorship? You could let me fuck your face."

With his cock still in my mouth, I moaned out my consent. Instantly, he took over, holding my head still while he raised his hips and thrust in over and over, plunging in deep, so deep that his tip hit the back of my throat.

My eyes watered, and I gagged. Still he drove in. I forced my throat to relax. I concentrated on breathing through my nose. I let myself enjoy being used. It wasn't hard to find the pleasure in it. It was so fucking hot. The hottest blow job I'd ever given, if it could still be called giving when he was so forcefully taking like he was. The roughness of it all added to the fantasy. It felt like I was "earning" something. It felt like I deserved to be given a reward.

It was such a turn-on that I thought I might come.

Scott was close to coming himself. I could feel the desperation in his strokes as his tempo became uneven. Just when I was preparing for him to spill, he pulled himself out. "Get on the couch, and spread your legs," he said as he dug into his pocket and pulled out a condom.

He'd known how this meeting would end up all along. At least we were on the same page.

Understanding where this was going, I rushed to do as he'd commanded, pulling my skirt to my waist as well.

He was still rolling the latex down over his cock when he spotted my bare pussy. "No panties?" He didn't sound disappointed.

"I figured I wouldn't leave with them even if I wore them in." Then I remembered we were playing the game. "I mean, I guess I forgot to put them on, Mr. Sebastian. Am I in trouble? Can I still earn your sponsorship?"

"So much trouble. Let's see if your pussy is worth what you want." He positioned himself above me, one knee on the sofa, the other foot still on the floor.

I gasped as he thrust in.

"Worth it," he said after a few strokes. "Completely fucking worth anything you want." He picked up the tempo to the one he'd used on my mouth. This, though, was very clearly about me. With his knee and one hand braced on the back of the sofa behind me, he moved the other down to play with my clit.

"You're so fun to play with, Tessa. The perfect little

168 | LAURELIN PAIGE

fuck toy. I almost wish you weren't so committed to being ethical so I could use you a whole bunch of ways before I let you get what you want. I would dirty you up so good. Make you never want to be fucked by anyone else ever again."

It was sex talk, filthy words that were said in the heat of the moment, the kind that always revved me up. If I was still capable of speech, I would have returned them in kind. *Dirty me up. Play with me all you want. I'll never fuck anyone who isn't you.*

It was possible I even meant it.

Luckily, my climax hit, followed immediately after by his, and I didn't have to wonder about the truth in my unspoken words. I was sure there wasn't any truth in his.

So why did I want to believe so badly that there was?

This was such a bad idea.

"Am I out of your system now?" I asked when he'd put himself away, disposed of the condom, and collapsed on the sofa next to me. I told myself I wanted the answer to be yes.

He didn't even hesitate. "No. Am I out of yours?"

"No." Just the opposite. He was like a drug. The more I had of him, the more I wanted him.

Which wasn't surprising since I had a pattern of falling for guys that had no desire to stick around. What was surprising was how there was still a part of me that wanted to believe Scott would be different.

I had to ignore that part of me.

And if I wanted to retain any self-dignity, I had to make some boundaries. Starting now.

I sat up and stared him in the eye. "Look, I know I'm the one who came in here offering sex. It was an immature move, one inspired by desperation. The DRF is really important to me."

"Yes. You'd do 'anything,'" he said, quoting my role play.

I tried not to smile and failed. Scott was fun. He was really fun. No doubt if I spent any more time with him, I'd get my heart broken. It was a good reason to walk away from him entirely.

But I wasn't going to walk away from the sponsorship.

And as long as I was there for that, Scott was going to be there too.

I wiped the smile from my face. "Scott, this can't happen—"

He sat up and sharply cut me off. "If you say this can't happen again—"

"This can't happen again until the contract is signed. We both have to agree to that. It's the only way we'll resist." It wasn't setting an impossible goal. It was doing the business first with the promise of fun later, like Teyana had suggested.

It was also hoping like hell that I made it to the fun before Kendra came back and ruined it all. All the more reason to concentrate on the job to be done.

I reached out and ran my fingers across Scott's bearded jaw. "I really don't want to screw this up."

He grabbed my hand and brought it to his lips, placing a soft kiss on my knuckle. "Fine. I'll agree." He stood up and tugged me to my feet as well. "Gives me incentive to

push this through. And you say you don't have the power."
He shook his head like it was the craziest thing he'd ever
heard.

He still didn't get it. Didn't get that any power I had
over him was a facade. Sure, he felt motivated by his dick
to move the vetting process along, but what was at stake
for him? Blue balls?

On the other hand, if he stalled this so long that I got
caught before the deal was signed, then I'd most likely be
out of a job, and the DRF would be out of a much-
needed sponsorship.

And Scott would hate me.

That last thing felt like the worst consequence of all.

FIFTEEN

Thursday afternoon, I stood with Sarah Boynton as she scanned the SIC conference room. It was a larger room than the one I'd met with the team in, more impressive. The furniture was top grade, and the entire back wall was floor-to-ceiling windows that offered a magnificent view of the Midtown skyline.

"I still can't believe you landed us with Sebastian Industrial," she said. "I keep pinching myself."

"This is just a coordination meeting. Let's not get ahead of ourselves." I reached over to knock on the conference table, which appeared to be made of real wood. While I was there, I straightened one of the Dysautonomia pamphlets that Sarah had set out when she'd first arrived, not that it needed it. Then I went about needlessly straightening all of them. I was fidgety with nerves and needed something to do with my hands, and I wasn't even the one who would be doing most of the talking today.

"Right, right." She followed behind me. "I want you to know I have no expectations. I'm appreciative that you've gotten us this far. After so long with no bites at all, I'd begun to wonder if our deal with Conscience Connect would lead anywhere at all."

If left to Kendra, probably not.

I didn't tell her that. "Setting up corporations with foundations is like dating. It can take a long time to find the right partner, but once you do, it can be magic."

"It's an honor to even get a date with SIC. Truly. Thank you again."

Satisfied with the pamphlet arrangement, I turned to Sarah. "You're welcome again." She'd already poured profuse gratitude on me when I'd called to set up the meeting on Monday after I'd left Scott's office. I didn't need to hear it, but it did remind me why I'd wanted to do this in the first place. It felt good to see the risk paying off.

"I'm even more thrilled that Kendra let you pitch it. I've been nudging her for months to give you the reins on this. Passion sells much better than any presentation, and you have it for the DRF."

"Well," I swallowed. Not for the first time, I considered telling her the truth. Sarah was the one who'd told me I had a job anytime I wanted at the DRF, and there was a good chance I'd need to take her up on that soon. Would telling her that I'd bucked authority to get this sponsorship put her off or impress her more?

The chance to confess disappeared when the conference doors opened and the first team members arrived, followed by SIC's lawyers, and then soon after, Eden leading in more representatives from the DRF. I busied myself with playing hostess, greeting everyone and passing on any beverage orders to Eden. Admittedly, I enjoyed ordering her around, probably more than I should.

At three p.m. on the dot, the doors opened again and Scott walked in.

And the air in my lungs went out.

I'd done a good job of putting him out of my head over the last few days, but at the sight of him, all the thoughts and feelings I'd repressed came flooding over me like a dam had been raised. My skin tingled in his presence. My lower belly hummed. My blood went warm, and I could feel color rising to my cheeks.

"Let's get started, please," he said as he crossed to the head of the table. Everyone scrambled to their seats, even those who had no idea who he was, because that was just who he was. The kind of command he held over a room.

It definitely was the kind of command he held over me.

Those blue eyes in particular held power over me, which was why I'd ordered myself to avoid eye contact at all costs during today's meeting. It was by pure accident that my gaze collided with his as I helped get everyone seated.

Hi, he mouthed, setting a thousand butterflies soaring in my stomach.

I fought a smile and lost. *Hi*, I mouthed back.

When I managed to pull my eyes away, I found Brett watching. He looked to Scott, then back to me. It didn't matter that Scott was now focused on the papers in front of him, Brett had seen our exchange, and his expression said he was not at all pleased.

It probably was fine. But his disapproval wiped the

smile from my lips and wound the butterflies in my tummy into a tight knot.

At least I wasn't sitting next to him since I was sure I'd get some sort of lecture whispered to me if I were. The spot that had been designated for me wasn't necessarily better, however, because it was next to Scott.

Okay, it was the best spot in the room, and when I'd realized I'd be sitting next to him, I'd done a mental happy dance. Usually, I spent these meetings across from him. Today, that space was left empty, a subtle reminder that of everyone gathered today, there was only one man in charge.

But sitting next to him had its drawbacks too. I could feel his body heat radiating off him. I could smell that dizzying woody scent of his. He was a distraction no matter what when I was in the room with him. Being so close only magnified his effect.

He, on the other hand, seemed completely unaffected. With as much professionalism and command as I'd ever seen from him, he launched into the business of conducting the meeting, introducing himself and giving a brief spiel about the company.

Seriously? Scott?

I glanced down at my phone as the incoming message from Brett flashed across the screen. Kicking myself for leaving it out in the first place, I started to turn it over.

But then the impulse to defend myself took over. What had he even witnessed? A greeting exchange. That was all. Never mind that more had occurred. Brett didn't know that.

> I shot a quick text back. I don't know what you're talking about.

> Don't play dumb with me. That look you gave him. I've seen that look before.

I glanced down the table and gave him a stern expression that I hoped said, *Come on, really?*

Only to realize that the whole room was watching me because apparently Scott had just turned the meeting over to me.

"Ah, yes, thank you, Scott," I said, quickly getting myself together. "I believe I've met everyone individually now, but in case I didn't, I'm Tess Turani. I'm here to be a liaison between Sebastian Industrial and the Dysautonomia Relief Foundation as we proceed. First up on the agenda is to discuss the ways that the DRF plans to spend any sponsorship monies received. With us today, we have several representatives from the DRF who will guide us through that."

Before I could proceed with introducing Sarah, the conference doors swung open again, and in walked Henry Sebastian.

If I'd thought Scott's entrance had been powerful, it paled in comparison to his father's. Henry took the room by force, as though he were at the center of a cyclone and everyone else bustled around him in his wind. Eden immediately rushed to get him water. Brett stood up to pull out the chair at the opposite end of the table. Silvia gathered the pamphlet in front of her and added it to the other materials I'd given her previously and set them in front of Henry's seat. Everyone else reacted too, sitting up straighter as though they were students and the principal had just walked in the room.

Even Scott seemed more alert. "I thought you hadn't planned to make it today," he said.

Henry didn't even look at him, flipping through the booklets in front of him instead. "I considered this important enough to shift my schedule around. If I'm going to sign a check for ten million, I intend to know what I'm getting out of it."

What *he* was getting out of it.

I forced myself not to roll my eyes. I knew as well as anyone that most corporations only gave in order to earn goodwill from the public.

Scott, on the other hand, felt the need to address it. "Not quite the attitude that's usually associated with charitable giving, Dad, but glad to have you. You should know what good the DRF is planning to do with those funds."

Without giving his father time to react to the subtle dig, he went on. "We were just getting to introductions. Carry on, Tess."

I had the distinct feeling that father and son were in the middle of a pissing contest, and the last thing I wanted to do was bring attention to myself.

But then I felt the warmth from Scott's lower leg as it pressed against mine under the table. I would have thought it accidental except that he kept it there, probably because he enjoyed the power games and got off on the idea of secretly fooling around, but I took it as a show of support.

It helped. Without missing a beat, I launched into introducing the members from the DRF, and when that was finished, I turned it over to Sarah to discuss the plans for the sponsorship funds.

"And who are you?" Henry interrupted before Sarah could say more than two words.

She blinked because hadn't he been listening? But she handled it graciously. "I'm Sarah Boynton. I'm the—"

Henry cut her off. "Not you. I mean you." His eyes locked directly on me.

Oh, yeah. He and I hadn't actually met. And he'd come in after my introduction. Of course he didn't know who I was.

Still, being put in the spotlight in such a way made my head light. Thank God for Scott's leg still pressed against mine. "I'm Tess Turani. I'm here as a liaison between SIC and the DRF."

Henry frowned, as though what I'd said didn't make sense to him.

"She's representing Conscience Connect," Scott explained.

Henry's frown relaxed, but he somehow didn't look any happier. "Why isn't Kendra Montgomery here herself?"

Oh, God. He knew Kendra too. Personally. Which, again, shouldn't have been a fucking surprise since she'd said the Sebastians were family friends. On the plus side, maybe it meant that was actually how she knew Scott and that they hadn't banged after all.

That plus was small consolation in the moment. I was convinced this was what I'd dreaded, that I was on the verge of being found out, and wouldn't it just be my luck to occur in such a public spectacle.

I wanted to crawl under the table.

"I don't know, Dad," Scott said, obviously annoyed. "Maybe she thought it was a conflict of interest. Whatever the reason, Tess has done an excellent job presenting options to the team. Kendra obviously sent her best, and we're lucky to have her."

I was the kind of girl who could turn praise like that into a declaration of love. Normally, I'd have been swooning at his feet.

Today, all it did was make me feel worse. Because Kendra hadn't sent her "best." She hadn't sent me at all.

And, oh God, Sarah was witnessing all of this. There went my backup job.

But then Henry nodded in acceptance. "Very well, then. Let's proceed."

My nerves didn't settle after that, even when the agenda was back on track. I was certain the whole meeting was a waste of time, that Henry Sebastian was bound to nix the whole thing. It hadn't occurred to me before then that Scott wasn't necessarily the final word when it came to placing the DRF with Sebastian Industrial. Now that I realized that the real power lay with a hard-hearted narcissist, I was positive there was no way the sponsorship would go through.

My fears seemed to be confirmed when, after everyone

at the DRF had spoken, Henry said, "I'm concerned that this organization is too feminist. Business is run by men. If we want to earn the respect of other businesses, we should be engaging with a foundation that benefits men."

All right. Now I was going to go off.

I had a myriad of things to say in response, starting with addressing that the idea that businesses were run by men was super outdated, followed by an in-depth tutorage on how anything that benefited women was a benefit to society as a whole, and ending with a long string of adjectives describing what a piece of shit he was.

Fortunately, the younger Sebastians were looking out for me.

A text flashed across my phone from Brett.
Don't do it.

At the same time, Scott addressed his father's asshole remarks. "It's hard to know where to begin to respond to that. The fallacies of thought hinted at in your statement are appalling and, to be frank, embarrassing, but I'm well aware that pointing them out will mean nothing to you. Instead, let me try to use language that you will hear—your current image has been tainted by a history of anti-feminist behavior. The attacks you've had in this area have increased in recent years. I know cleaning up that perception is not your priority, but doing so would definitely get the attention of the press. You want to draw focus away from the other messy parts of SIC? Then my advice is to endorse a female-centric foundation, and let the public praise you for your reform. No one has to know it's only for show."

The room was quiet. Tension stretched from one side of the table to the next, a blanket so thick it was hard to breathe.

Both Scott and Henry seemed completely unconcerned, as though scathing conversations were conducted between the two of them in front of others on a daily basis. Maybe they were. I'd never been in a meeting with them both before. What did I know?

To Scott's credit, though his words had been biting, his tone had been matter-of-fact. While I'd been well aware of his ability to lead, this was the first time I'd really seen him acting in his role as VP of image. These were probably the things he advised his father and the board on all the time. Perhaps the questions he'd asked during our meetings hadn't been just to stall but also so he'd be equipped to handle Henry Sebastian.

I imagined it would be hard to constantly have to confront his father like this. It was possibly me projecting—I would never dream of having hard words with my dad. Of course, since my father hadn't spoken to me in fifteen years, any words with him at all were hard to imagine.

Still, I felt for Scott. Even though he appeared stoic and untouched, I pressed my leg harder against his, wanting to give him the same show of support he'd shown me. And to thank him, for sticking up for the DRF when he could have presented him with something else.

He glanced at me in response, his expression serious. His eyes, though, said something I couldn't quite read, something I was sure was just for me.

Well, at least I had that. When I was out of a job and a

laughingstock in the community, I'd remember that look. Maybe all I was about to lose would even be worth it because of that one glance.

After what felt like a lifetime, Henry finally responded. "That gives me much to think about. I'll consider it in my decision." He stood, doing up his jacket button as he did. "We'll get back to you soon."

He left the room as abruptly as he entered.

The floor felt like it was dropping out from under me. Coordination meetings were supposed to be a matter of formality, and here we were going to have to leave with the partnership unconfirmed.

Sarah turned to me, disappointment in her eyes.

I'll fix this, my eyes said in return. But it was a promise I had no business making.

Meanwhile, everyone at the table seemed confused. A few people shuffled, not knowing if the meeting was over or not.

Brett attempted to settle the question. "Should we—"

Scott cut him off. "We'll go ahead and have the contracts prepared," he said, eyeing the lawyers present. "SIC has very specific image issues that need to be addressed with the foundation we sponsor. There is no better choice than the DRF for this, and though my father isn't yet convinced, I guarantee you he will be."

It was hard not to look at him then as a hero, hard not to feel something tight and warm in my chest at his gallant declaration of support.

But I couldn't help wondering if Scott was also making promises he had no business making.

SIXTEEN

Scott wrapped up the meeting after his bold declaration and left the room at the same quick pace as his father.

My whole body felt heavy. There had never been a chance that I'd walk out of today with signed contracts—they still had to be written, details negotiated—but it should have felt like a done deal. Even with Scott's promise, it seemed like that was miles away, disappearing into the horizon.

I needed a drink.

Before I could drown my sorrows, however, I had to finish doing my job, er, the one I'd created for myself.

"Sarah," I said, rushing over to her. "I'm so sorry about this. I hadn't been informed that Henry Sebastian had to put his stamp of approval on this, or I would have met with him before bringing you in. I'm truly embarrassed by all this."

She looked nowhere as disheartened as I felt, and on top of that she appeared baffled. "Embarrassed about the

Sebastians drawing up contracts for a partnership? I'm pleased we're getting that far."

Had she not been in the same room I'd been in?

"They haven't indicated they'll sign yet, though. And Henry was…" I wanted to say an asshole but decided it wouldn't be the most professional thing to call him. "Well, he was awfully callous about an organization that does an extreme amount of good."

She made a dismissive tsk with her tongue. "You think he's the first CEO who has suggested that the reason dysautonomia doesn't get funded is because it's a disease that happens to women? I wish. He's not even the tenth. Believe it or not, we generally walk away with a check of some kind once we make it to this point. If it's not the sponsorship, that will be disappointing, but it will likely be a sizable donation, and no way am I going to consider that a loss."

I had a hard time being so optimistic. Sure, a donation was a donation, and the charity always needed funds. But it wasn't just about the money. A corporate sponsorship would bring awareness to a common ailment that many people knew very little about.

And on a personal basis, there was no way that Kendra would overlook my going behind her back if I didn't walk away with a coup. It was probably a good time to plant a seed about needing a job with Sarah.

Except, when I opened my mouth, I couldn't bring myself to say it. I hadn't really wanted to leave Conscience Connect when this started, and now that I'd done some actual pitching, I wanted to leave even less. And not just because I felt some stupid loyalty to Kendra—that loyalty was so thin these days, it was almost a deterrent. I wanted to stay because I believed in the work. There were a lot of organizations I felt passionately about, not just the DRF. I wanted to find sponsors for all of them.

Which was why I wasn't giving up hope.

"You're right, Sarah. Any donation would be fantastic, but my job is to get you a sponsorship, and by damn, I'm gonna do that."

She broke into a smile. "When you say it like that, I have no choice but to believe you."

Most of the room had emptied by this point, and I still needed to clean up. Sarah offered to help, but I shooed her out with a promise to keep her updated. When she'd gone, I was alone except for Brett.

From the judgy look on his face, he hadn't stayed to help.

"You saw us exchange one smile," I said, exasperated. "I'm not sure how you could draw any conclusions from that."

"I know my cousin."

"Second cousin," I corrected, as though the difference mattered, and began gathering the leftover pamphlets from the conference table.

Brett followed me around. "Still family. Still have spent lots of time with the guy. Still familiar with how he is with women, and not to be disrespectful to the man, he's not very nice."

So far, Scott Sebastian had been plenty nice to me.

But I knew what he meant.

"I'll take your warning to heart," I said, which wasn't exactly a lie since I'd already been warning myself the same thing for days.

Brett wasn't satisfied. "Tess…"

I stopped my work and turned toward him. "What? He's a player. I got it. I'll try to make sure I don't smile at him again." In public, anyway.

"I'm serious here. He's got a reputation for stringing girls along, even when he knows that they're misinterpreting his actions."

Scott had probably done that to a lot of girls, but I suddenly had a strong feeling Brett was talking about Eden. Hadn't Scott mentioned Brett was her friend? After witnessing the way Scott had been with her, I could see how she'd feel strung along. Brett probably harbored resentment toward Scott over that. Especially if he liked me as I had a feeling he did.

I didn't need him to protect me, though. I liked owning my mistakes all out. "That sucks that he does that," I said. "It really does. I've been on the other end of that more times than I'd like to count."

"Then you understand what I'm saying."

"I do. And you understand that I'm saying I get it. I know what you're trying to warn me about. I appreciate you looking out for me." I gave him a reassuring smile. "But I can handle myself. I promise."

It wasn't what he'd wanted, I was sure. He'd wanted me to say I'd stay away from Scott altogether. I wouldn't do that. I couldn't.

But it was all over his face as he studied me. I knew

what he was thinking, too, because I'd thought it myself a million times. Why would a girl knowingly get mixed up with a heartbreaker? Why wouldn't she pick a decent man who treated women with respect?

Good question, Brett. Damned if I know.

He seemed to come to his own damning conclusion. "If you think you need to get with him to get this contract…"

Now I was all sorts of offended. I'd gone out of my way with Scott to be sure that I didn't get accused of crossing ethical lines, and here Brett was suggesting it anyway. Based on a smile, no less. Is that really what he thought of me?

And why jump to that conclusion at all? Couldn't I be interested in flirting with a player because I didn't mind being played? Were women not allowed to have drive-by sex the way men did?

My indignation must have shown on my face.

"I'm sorry. I shouldn't have suggested that you'd do something like that. I just wanted you to know, in case he pressured you…"

"Has he been known to do that?" It was one thing for Scott to be a philanderer. If he purposefully used his power over women, that was another thing.

"No, he hasn't," Brett admitted. "That doesn't mean I'd put it past him."

He really was sour about his cousin. Second cousin.

I hesitated before responding as I replayed all my interactions with Scott so far, looking for any breach of ethics on his part. I couldn't find any besides the ones I'd already known about, and I was just as much a party to those as he'd been. It was a good thing we'd agreed to put a hold on whatever it was we were doing until the contracts were signed, just to be sure.

Though, I was already longing for him way more than I cared to admit.

"Scott has been very professional," I assured Brett. "And as much as I want SIC to sponsor the DRF, I wouldn't use sex to go about it." Role-playing it was a different story.

"Okay. I'm reassured. I was only trying to look out for you. Not trying to assume the worst."

"I know. Thank you. I've got it under control."

He nodded. Then we stood there awkwardly, neither of us sure what to say next.

"I should finish..." I gestured to the pile of pamphlets in my hand.

"Of course. Do you need help?"

I was nearly done, and even if I weren't, I was ready to be by myself. "Nope. I got it."

After he left, I threw the pamphlets into my briefcase, gathered up the few bits of trash that had been left, and sighed. I had no idea if anyone else had the room booked after, which was why I should have been scurrying to get out of there, but my head was overwhelmed, and I needed a minute. There was too much to sort out between worrying if Henry would nix the deal and if I'd have a job when Kendra came back and what to do with my new found passion for selling causes if I was fired and wondering if Brett's concern about Scott meant he was even more of a player than I'd realized.

So instead of trying to sort anything, I placed my palms on the conference table, and took a deep breath, and let myself be okay with all the unknowns.

And tried very hard not to imagine Scott pushing me down further and fucking me from behind.

Since, of course, that was exactly what I was thinking about the most, I jumped back like I'd been doing something naughty when I heard the sound of the door opening. Probably someone else needed the room.

"Just leaving!" I turned to grab my briefcase from the chair, then dropped it back in the chair when I looked up and saw who'd entered.

"I was hoping you'd still be here," Scott said, his blue eyes latching with mine. His tie matched the color exactly, I realized now. As well as his cufflinks, which was somehow really sexy.

He really was too hot to look at in general. Not without repercussions, anyway. Like storms of butterflies in my stomach and goosebumps skipping down my skin and panties that were suddenly flooded.

And I shouldn't have been as thrilled as I was that he'd come looking for me. Especially when he most definitely shouldn't have been looking for me.

So much for having this thing with Scott under control.

"You just caught me," I said, hoping my voice didn't sound as shaky as I felt. "What's up?"

"I wanted to apologize for my father. I invited him as a formality. He never follows through on those invitations. I didn't think he'd show up this time, or I would have warned you."

Oh. It was about business then.

Stupid me, I was disappointed.

No, this was good. Business talk was perfectly accept-able. "I'll admit, I was taken aback by him. Mostly, I was caught off guard by the realization that he's the one who ultimately decides if this goes through or not."

"Yes, he is," he confirmed. "For that matter, he's the final say on everything SIC does. He just doesn't typically concern himself with most of it. I'm not sure why he de-cided to poke his head in this time. He probably thought I was taking too long to get the deal done."

"Wonder why he would think that?"

He gave the slightest of smiles. "Whatever the reason, there's nothing to worry about. He'll come around. This is his way. He doesn't like to appear like he's giving anything easily."

It didn't make me feel any more confident that this would end up okay, but I wasn't really interested in think-ing about that at the moment.

"Oh, is that where you learned it?" I teased. It was too easy not to. Too much of a temptation to try to lure another smile.

I didn't get one this time. Instead, he feigned offense. "I'm not like that."

"*Difficult* is the word I was told about you." I told my-self I wasn't worried about Brett's more recent warnings.

Scott gave a huh sound. "Difficult," he mused. "I'm glad I keep Brett on his toes."

"Among other people."

He'd moved closer at some point. Or I had. Now he

was only an arm's length away. I could reach my hand out and yank him to me if I wanted to.

The thought somehow circled me back to an earlier one. "You know, if your dad is really the last word on the matter, then what's happened between us couldn't really be considered unethical since you don't have any power to hold over me in the first place."

He winced a little. "I wouldn't say I don't have *any* power."

"Sorry," I laughed. "Did I insult your manhood?"

"My manhood is fine, thank you very much. I was simply making sure you were clear on the facts."

"Crystal clear now. I appreciate the clarification. And I wasn't trying to diminish your position. I was making myself feel better."

"And do you? Feel better?" His voice was low, and suggestive. He'd inched closer again, too.

Or I had, which wouldn't be surprising considering that I was also now putting together that if I had no reason to feel better about what we'd done in the past, then there wasn't much reason to keep from doing it again.

I wondered if he was thinking the same thing.

As if he could read my thoughts, he said, "By the way, I locked the door."

There were so many other reasons not to lunge myself at him, reasons beyond the ethics of the situation, like the fact that he was probably a bigger player than I'd first thought and the fact that we were in the conference room of his work.

But I'd seemed to have a strained relationship with

reason since I'd met Scott Sebastian, so a couple of minutes later, I found my back against the window, one leg wrapped around his thigh, his erection rubbing against my belly as he kissed me like a starving man.

"Turn around," he said when he broke away to breathe.

I did as he said, the view from being pressed right against the window giving me a flash of vertigo. I blinked, and with the world righted, I realized how kinky this was. We were much too high to be seen from the sidewalk and too far from the building across the street for anyone to be able to tell what we were doing if they looked. But it certainly felt like we were on display in front of the whole of Midtown, and that was super crazy hot. Much better than the banging on the conference table.

"God, yes," I said, undoing my dress pants and pushing them to my ankles along with my panties.

"Of course you're an exhibitionist. I knew you were perfect, Tessa." I heard the rip of the condom, which he must have put on at lightning speed because it was barely a handful of seconds later that he lined his tip up to my hole and shoved in.

"Fuck, Scott." Even with my bra on, my breasts bounced against the glass. His tempo was merciless. "Just...fuck."

"I haven't been able to stop thinking about your pussy. I convinced myself I didn't remember it right. It couldn't feel that good. Fucking you couldn't feel that good."

"And does it?"

"It feels so much fucking better."

"It does, it does, it does." It couldn't decide if I was crushed that it did because I really didn't need to get addicted to the man's cock or if I was elated that he felt the same because I was already completely addicted and had to have him a whole bunch more times in a whole bunch more places.

I was both. Both crushed and elated and really, really turned on. By all of it—the sneaking around and the borderline ethics and the banging against the glass in broad daylight. "Do you think anyone can see us?"

He nipped at my ear before answering. "If they can, no one can tell what we're doing. Unless they have binoculars."

My pussy clenched down around him. "Obviously, I'm pretending that someone does."

He let out a growl. "Perfection. Fucking perfection."

Perfection. That's exactly what it was. His speed, his angle, his girth, his length. The way he hit that exact right spot. Each. And. Every. Time. The way he called me Tessa, and the way he smiled when he saw me, and the way his eyes lit up when they met mine.

It should have frightened my climax away to realize I was thinking about him on a level that went beyond just sex, but that seemed instead to be the thing that brought it on. It tore through me like a tornado, twisting my insides and making my head spin and sending dots flying across my vision like debris caught in the storm.

"Yes, yes, yes," Scott said under his breath as he continued to saw into me, the last *yes* drawn out when his body stiffened and he trembled out his release.

Actually, I thought it was my name he was clinging to. "Tessa, Tessa, Tesssssssa." But I didn't want to acknowledge that. Not when I was already so close to losing sight of what this was between us, what this had to be to me because of what it most surely was for him—sex and nothing more. Sweet words didn't change that. The way he said my name didn't change that.

He stayed inside me while he regained control of his breath. When he pulled out, he immediately turned me around to face him, catching me when I stumbled over the pants wrapped at my ankles. A skirt would have been easier, but at least he wouldn't be able to steal my panties this time.

I wasn't sure I considered that a win.

"Have dinner with me tomorrow night," he said. He kissed me before I could answer, less urgent than before but just as committed. "My place. Seven. Don't say no."

My heart was racing. Experienced as I was with players, I was well aware that this was when I needed to cut this off. "Okay, I won't say no."

Knowing the right thing and doing it were two very different things.

He narrowed his eyes, as though he didn't trust me. "Don't say maybe, either. Say you'll be there. I need you to be there."

"I'll be there." As if I would ever have given any other answer.

"Good girl." His smile was victorious. "Next time I fuck you, it's going to be in a bed."

SEVENTEEN

I stood at the threshold between Scott's living room and his balcony and gaped. "This is one hell of a fuck pad."

I'd thought his apartment had been high-end. Turned out I hadn't even seen the best part. The balcony extended the entire length of his apartment with a door coming from the main area and another from the bedroom, and with the size and furnishings, it basically added another functional living space. A round dining table set was positioned in front of a long rectangular electric fireplace, which had been turned on, thankfully, since the night had gotten chilly. Several oversize patio chairs filled the space, most with accompanying ottomans, but the real focus piece was the couch that was big enough to be a bed.

Considering that the balcony was completely walled off from the neighbors on both sides, I had no doubt the couch had been used as such. It was how I'd use it if it had been mine, anyway.

"I can't tell if you're praising or judging," Scott said, coming up beside me.

I wouldn't tell him there was a third option that involved complicated feelings of jealousy and unworth. "Neither. I'm trying to figure out if this is a booty call or a date."

"Is there a difference?"

"That tells me all I need to know." It was what I needed to remember too—Scott Sebastian did not do dates. He did sex. Lots and lots of sex, and he did it pretty damn well, probably *because* he was so practiced.

I wished the reminder didn't make me feel so gutted.

I wrapped the lace shawl I'd borrowed from Kendra's closet tighter around the rose floral print satin maxi (also borrowed and crossed over to the fireplace, hoping it looked like I was trying to get warm rather than get away from him.

It wasn't that I wanted to be away from him per se. It was that I wanted to be away from my increasingly complex feelings about him, and of course there was nowhere to get away from those. Wherever I went, there I was and all that.

And wherever he went, there he was, gorgeous and sexy and unattainable. I didn't have to look at him to remember just how much of each of those qualities he was.

"I suppose this is when I should deliver my spiel."

I turned to look at him and raised both brows in question. I'd sadly never been able to do just one the way Tey did.

"The spiel where I explain that I don't do commitment, don't get attached, this is all fun for fun's sake, no hard feelings, it's who I am."

It was insane how he could make the after-work look so appealing without even trying. His hair was mussed, his tie gone, his shirt unbuttoned at the collar, his hands stuck in his pockets all casual-like.

And yes, right, he's in the middle of telling me not to fall for him. I should pay attention.

"But..." he continued, then trailed off.

"But you realized I already know all of that because of the circumstances under which we met?"

"There is that. I was going to say but I realized I don't... want to."

I had to force myself to breathe. There were so many ways I could insert meaning into those words. It could also be a well-practiced line.

More likely it was the latter. "That's terribly smooth of you."

"This time I'm sure it's not a compliment."

I glanced away, unable to take the intensity of his gaze. "I don't know what it is. A warning to myself for self-preservation."

"I can't blame you. But I wish you didn't feel that way."

He sure knew how to draw my eyes back to him. I studied him this time, looking for any signs of insincerity. I needed proof to show my heart. *See, look, you fool, you. He's rehearsed this. It doesn't mean anything.*

When I didn't find anything that confirmed what I needed it to, I decided it was time to get off shaky ground. "I think I'm maybe not ready for conversations that discuss feelings. Is that wine I spy?"

"There is wine, yes." He moved to pour it into the glasses already set out on the table that was decked out as though we were at a five-star restaurant instead of his luxury apartment balcony. A long cream cloth covered it. Candles were lit, the wine chilled in a bucket with ice. Stainless-steel covered plates adorned the side buffet.

Several plates, actually. Was he expecting more guests?

He anticipated the question. "I didn't ask about your food preferences so I had my chef make a few different things." He handed me my wine glass so his was free to lift up the lids on the various dishes. "Eggplant parmigiana. Lasagna bolognese. Garden salad—seeds instead of croutons in case you don't do gluten. Grilled shrimp. Caprese."

"Will you think bad thoughts about me if I have a little bit of each?"

"I'll think bad thoughts about you either way."

"I hope so." My smile broke through without warning. It felt like it was revealing too much, for some reason, so I let it fade. "Italian is a favorite of mine. You chose well."

I was probably imagining it, but his cheeks seemed to pink, and I suddenly had the impression that he didn't normally do this for a woman. That he didn't consider her tastes. That he ordered for himself and/or to show off.

At least, that had been my experience with the players I'd dated in the past. No one had ever put this much thought into serving me, not after they'd gotten into my panties, anyway.

It was a dangerous thought, one I shouldn't think about too long, so I concentrated on my wine and directed Scott with what to load on my plate instead.

The food was to die for, every bite better than the last, which was surprising considering how simple the menu was. I probably spent an entire ten minutes complimenting each item—in orgasmic fashion, as Scott pointed out—leaving little need to worry about trivial small talk.

But then my enthusiasm for the food waned as my belly filled, and silence crept in. Not the awkward kind, just the kind that invited conversation.

"Tell me about yourself, Tessa," he said when the quiet had begun to linger too long.

I blinked at him in horror. "I'm having sudden flashbacks to every awful Match.com date I've ever been on. Why would you ask such a banal thing?"

"I was attempting to differentiate between a date and a booty call. Though, you must clarify—is there still booty involved in your version of a date?"

"As long as it doesn't involve generic conversation starters like *tell me about yourself.*"

His laugh turned my insides to jelly. "I guess it's obvious now that I'm more skilled at getting to know women in the biblical way."

"Oh, it was obvious before."

There was potential to turn the talk dirty from there, and I wouldn't have minded in the slightest.

Instead, Scott became somber. "I really do want to know you though, Tessa. I'll try better to make it as painless as possible." He thought for a second. "What's Tess short for? Theresa?"

Ah, fuck. We were really doing this. It occurred to me that the whole reason I was into the love 'em and leave 'em types was specifically so I wouldn't ever be forced to talk about myself.

This question wasn't hard, though. "Terese."

"Terese Turani." He said it like he was savoring the taste, the same way I'd savored the eggplant parmigiana. "Is there a middle name?"

"Nope." I almost left it there. Then I kicked myself. If he was going to make the effort, I could as well. "My father was Iranian, and middle names aren't a normal part of the culture, and I don't think my mother cared enough to argue it."

I saw the moment it clicked, the oh-so familiar realization of *yes, that's why I get an ethnic vibe about her.* I'd gotten it all my life.

"Iranian," he said as the dots connected. *"Shomâ Fârsi sohbat mekunid?"*

Now that was new. Usually, only other brownish peo-ple tried to engage in the language. Never one of the white guys. "I have no idea what you just said, but I'm guessing it was Farsi, and whoa, that was extremely hot."

"I asked if you speak Farsi, which is about the only phrase in Persian that I know. Sorry to disappoint."

"Do you know other languages?"

"Spanish. German. Some French."

"Then still extremely hot."

His foot wrapped around my ankle under the table, as though claiming it as his. "How about you?"

"Oh, I'm extremely hot as well."

"You don't need to tell me." His eyes drifted to my bo-som. I imagined the dress was more revealing on me than

Kendra since she wasn't quite as busty as I was. I'd chosen it for exactly that reason.

The heat behind his gaze said Scott approved.

"But I meant languages." Apparently he didn't approve enough to abandon the "getting to know you" dialogue.

I decided it was time to change the setting.

Setting my cloth napkin on top of my dish, I stood with my wine glass and headed toward the couch/bed. "I speak English, obviously, and I'm not the worst at Spanish, but I'm nowhere near able to converse in it."

As I'd hoped, he followed. "We could practice."

"Not if you want to get laid."

"No Spanish then."

I smiled triumphantly then sat down and arranged myself into what I hoped was an inviting pose. Seduction hadn't been necessary so far with Scott. It felt a little strange to have to try.

I needn't have worried. He stretched out in the spot I wanted him, right next to me, propping himself up on his side, his entire body angled toward me.

I would have thought the new seating arrangement would have ended all serious talk. I was wrong.

"So your father was Iranian, but you don't speak any Farsi—not a good relationship with Dad?"

I took a sip of the cabernet to buy me time to decide how to respond. I didn't have to answer. I could distract him instead.

Weirdly, when I'd swallowed, I found I wanted to talk about it. "He and my mother were never married. They sort of did the common law thing for a minute, but they broke up when I was four. Besides sending child support, he was never the best at staying involved after that, and then when he got married later on it was like the string was cut all together. As though it was an either/or type of deal. Like he had to choose between her and me, and he chose her. I haven't spoken to him since. I think I was twelve?"

"I'm sorry. That must have been hard for you."

I shrugged like it hadn't hurt as much as it had. Like it didn't still hurt. "My mother married the year before I graduated high school. A little late for a father figure, but he's a good man. He fills the role well enough."

I regretted it as soon as I'd said it. Not because it wasn't true—Bruce was a good man, and for all intents and purposes, he did fill the role of what I imagined a father should be. He'd taught me to change a tire and balance a checkbook. He gave the "respect my girl" speech to my prom date.

But that wasn't all the truth. It *had* been hard for me to be fatherless—envying friends who got to go to daddy-daughter dances, always feeling as though no matter what I did or accomplished, I had failed at keeping the interest of the one man that should have been easiest to win over.

It had been hard, too, to be inextricably tied to a culture that I knew absolutely nothing about. Sure, I could have learned about Iran on my own, but that wasn't the same as learning it from someone who lived it.

Wanting for some reason to share more, I chose that to expand on since it was the easier thing to admit. "It would have been nice to have someone to talk to about the experiences that come with having a Persian name and Persian coloring. Someone who could relate, I mean. Like, I get pulled out of every airport security line for a 'random' pat-down. And every time someone hears Turani they have to ask about my ethnicity. Which is also a weird thing because I'm white, right? But I'm also 'other,' and there's no box to mark it on any of the forms, so where does that leave me? Minor inconveniences. I'm not complaining that I'm treated unfairly. It would just be nice to have someone in my life who has the same experiences."

I shook my head, realizing the fault in the desire. "Of course, my father was born and raised in Iran, is much darker than me, has the accent, and practices the culture. His experiences are probably nothing like mine."

"But it would be nice to know."

"I guess it would be nice to know him period."

Scott ran his hand lazily down my torso, over my hips to my thighs and back again. "I don't know. If he's anything like my father, you may be better off not knowing him."

"Not knowing your father would mean not knowing this life."

"Would probably be worth the exchange."

His touch was distracting, but not so distracting that I didn't catch that he was looking for sympathy. Now this was like the players I'd met before. "Is the rich, white boy boohooing about his rich, white life?"

"Hey, that's a little unfair." His hand stopped its journey, but it settled on my hip so I didn't mind too much. "I acknowledge that I'm privileged, yes. It doesn't mean that every day is all jet planes and champagne. I don't get everything I want. I have obligations that feel oppressive."

"Such as?" It was hard to believe he really knew oppression. The glimpses I'd had into Kendra's life seemed to show that money might not buy everything, but it sure bought freedom.

He didn't even have to think about it. "My job, for one. If I'd wanted to be a doctor or a lawyer or an entertainer, I would have been disowned. The only choice for me was to go into the family business. My path has been laid out from the day I was born, whether I agree or not. SIC is the source of any money I hope to inherit, and that means I have to 'put in the time,' according to my father. So here I am, VP of Image and Outreach, which was not my first choice. Not even my tenth choice. But it's my title because PR is where my father wanted me so now I'm stuck there until he decides I'm worthy of something better."

I could see it would be hard to walk away from the lifestyle he'd gotten used to, but if he did, he'd still probably be better off than most people I knew. In other words, he still had a choice.

I had a feeling bringing that up would be too confrontational for a first date, though, and definitely off limits for any booty call.

I chose another aspect of his speech to remark on. "Careful. My degree is in PR."

His eyes widened as if he realized something he hadn't before. "That suddenly makes sense." He seemed to tuck that thought away and changed gears. "My degree is in business, and I'm not dismissing public relations as a career. I'd maybe even enjoy it in another situation. It's one thing to sell a company or a product that can bring good into the world or make lives easier or provide entertainment. It's another to have to convince people that the man behind the company is not a complete piece of shit, contrary to the evidence."

That did sound icky, and it occurred to me that his life might be more complicated than I gave him credit for. "I'm lucky that I get to sell things I believe in, I suppose."

"You are."

His hand began its sweep again, up and down, sending goosebumps scattering down my arms. His eyes darted to my breasts. To my lips. I wet them in anticipation.

Then, just when I thought he might lean in, I drew back. "What did you mean that it makes sense that I'm in PR?"

"You work with Kendra. She has the same degree."

The mention of my boss made my body tense. I threw back the rest of my wine, then twisted to set the glass down on the ground. And so that I wouldn't have to look at him when I responded. "Yeah. That's how we met, actually. Georgetown. We were in the same class."

"Impressive. I was forced to go to Columbia since Dad insisted I be able to intern for him at the same time."

That drew my head back so I could give him an incredulous stare. "Now you're crying about Columbia?"

"I'm not crying about anything. I'm telling you my life."

"Fair, fair."

"So you met Kendra at school, and that's how you ended up working with her?"

My skin felt itchy, and I was restless. I wanted to stand

up and walk away—from the topic, from the anxiety of my untruths, from the vulnerability of sharing. But like before, I knew they weren't things I could escape.

So I stayed. "We were friends first," I said carefully. "Teyana too. The three of us were thick as thieves the whole time we were there. So after college, when I was desperate for a job, and Conscience Connect was up and running, Kendra offered me a position. I think it was her way of showing she cared."

"It's very Montgomery to throw money in place of feelings."

"I've learned that about her." I'd used that excuse to justify her actions time and time again. She knew how to write a check. She didn't know how to truly love. Her heart was in the right place, she just didn't know how to show it.

Sometimes I blamed myself for that. I'd thought I could change that about her somehow.

"I take it you aren't close anymore?"

"Business relationships change things," I said.

"Not always, but yes. Sometimes they do."

It was an invitation to say more, and part of me wanted to even, but I couldn't get into that with Scott. I'd have to explain my real relationship with Kendra, confess that I was just her errand girl rather than someone she trusted to share the real work. We were already on dangerous grounds just talking about her at all, especially when I had so little to go on about his own association with her.

My brow furrowed. "What about you? How well do you know Kendra?"

"Uh." His hand dropped from my hip, making him feel

like he'd moved a million miles away. He ran it through his hair. "Our parents are...friends. It doesn't seem the right word considering how superficial their interactions are, but I think that's how they would label the relationship."

"And your relationship with Kendra is also superficial?"

"It's not what I'd call a relationship at all, honestly." He was evasive, his eyes shifting everywhere.

The truth was apparent, but I had to know, once and for all. "Have you slept with her?"

A guilty grin broke out across his face. "I've fucked her. Yes."

"Figured as much." I was suddenly grateful that Kendra's separation of jobs and men went both ways, otherwise I'd be worried he knew more about me and my position at Conscience Connect than he let on.

Actually, even if Kendra were less of a compartmentalist, I probably wouldn't be that worried about it because I was too preoccupied with the fact that Scott had indeed fucked my boss. That Kendra had been naked with him before I had. That, as always, she got first dibs, and I was left with the scraps.

Not that any of my interactions with Scott could be equated to scraps.

"Does it bother you?" His eyes twinkled, as though he found the question amusing.

I wasn't sure if I exactly understood it. "Bother?"

"I thought it would be easier to admit to being bothered than jealous."

It pricked at me because it was so spot-on. I hated that

he could see me so clearly.

So, of course, I deflected. "You really think a lot of yourself, don't you?"

"I think it's actually an indication of what I think about you. What I hope about you." His hand was back, just a finger this time, tracing along the strap of my dress, sending a shiver down my spine.

How could I resist when he touched me? "I'm a little jealous."

"Good. I'm glad."

I wanted to ask more about his fucking/non-relationship with Kendra—how long it had gone on, when it ended, who'd broken it off with whom—but I also didn't want to know.

Besides, it didn't matter in the moment because she was who knows where, wrapped up in herself while I was here, with Scott wrapped up in me.

"I don't want to talk about Kendra anymore," I said, leaning in.

"I hope you don't want to talk at all."

"I don't." But my words were lost to the mind-numbing, delicious pressure of his kiss.

EIGHTEEN

Kissing became more than kissing pretty fast, as was to be expected considering our track record. Even so, it wasn't as urgent as usual, which made sense since we weren't in a car or an office or a conference room. We knew there was time, so the only thing rushing us was our need, and need now was as much about exploring as it was about getting to the climax.

While it became more than kissing—hands wandering, hips grinding—the kissing didn't stop. We really hadn't done much kissing before this, and he seemed as uneager to rush it as I was. He lingered on my mouth, his tongue moving in and out at a languid pace, taunting me with promises of how he intended to treat me with his cock. How he intended to fuck me slowly and well and thoroughly.

When he eventually moved from my lips, he trailed kisses elsewhere, on my face, on my neck, on my collarbone, not only tasting but savoring each part of my body. I found myself torn between trying to learn him as well and simply enjoying what he was doing to me. I fought to do both at irst, sneaking in nibbles at his ear, then throwing my head back in ecstasy as his hand fondled my breast. Discovering he really liked it when I bit his neck, and then letting him see how much I liked it in return.

Soon, I was too overwhelmed with sensation to concentrate on delivering my best self, and I surrendered to being completely and utterly ravished.

"I'm dying to see these," he said after sucking my nipple to a sharp point underneath the silk dress. I'd had to go sans bra because of the open back, which had almost made me change my mind about wearing that outfit at all. Now I was glad since I knew the added layer of material would have diminished this particular moment.

Though, of course, I could always lose the dress all together.

But not yet. I wasn't ready to move from this spot to make that happen, and I was admittedly greedy for the same attention on the other breast.

"You've seen them," I reminded him. I turned slightly, offering it up to his mouth, an invitation he took readily. "I woke up naked in your bed last time, and I do not believe I was the one who undressed me."

"Mm." The hum of the sound vibrated against my breast, shooting sparks of ecstasy to my pussy. He persisted with his sucking for so long I almost forgot what we'd been talking about when he spoke again. "I kept my eyes closed."

I laughed. "You did not."

"I might have peeked." He clamped his teeth around

my nipple and pulled, turning my laugh into a gasp of pleasure. "Definitely not enough time to truly appreciate them. I'm going insane imagining them bare and primed like this."

"Then maybe you should do something about that." I started to roll over so that he could access the zipper at my lower back, but he stopped me.

"While I am entirely into your esteem for exhibitionism, I have to insist that you keep them put away out here. We have privacy for the most part, but there has been an occasional shot taken from the paparazzi." His mouth moved south, loitering at my belly button when he found it.

The threat of paparazzi momentarily threw me out of the zone as it reminded me of how different our worlds were. Kendra had a swanky balcony, and even she wasn't of the kind of money that precluded sunbathing nude.

But it was a very small moment of distraction. Because the threat of paparazzi was kind of exciting. I definitely didn't want to be photographed for all the world with my bits hanging out, but to think that we were potentially being watched? It was as hot on his balcony as it had been against the window in his office building.

I played the idea up in my head. "So you want to see me naked, but you're resisting from tearing my clothes off because of the need to protect me?" It didn't matter that I was a woman who could take care of herself—I would always get off on a man defending my honor. "Something like that?"

"Exactly like that."

I moaned, the details of this fantasy heightening my

need.

"I know, Tessa. I'm going to take care of you."

God, it was like he could read my mind.

He slunk lower, his head blocking the view to any potential onlookers as he pushed my dress up around my waist. "Once again, no panties, no bra. You seem to like to make this easy for me."

"I prefer not to add to your collection of women's underwear."

He rubbed his nose down my slit, inhaling as he did. "I don't collect women's underwear."

I made a sound that was half harumph and half ohmygod, ohmygod because he very obviously did collect women's underwear, but it was hard to argue anything with him when his tongue was doing that thing it was to my hole.

He seemed to discern my disbelief anyway. "I don't. I collect *your* underwear. That's all."

This statement was even more unbelievable than the last, and I propped myself up on my elbows, ready to dispute it. It was definitely not the kind of comment I could leave without remark. He was a player. I knew that going in. I was okay with it going in. I would *not* be okay with it if he pretended this thing between us was anything other than it was.

Actually, I might not be okay in the end even if he acknowledged the truth of the situation, but that was on me, not him, and the only chance I had of not getting completely wrecked over him was if he remained as transparent as possible.

But now his finger was tracing the rim of my pussy and

his tongue was flicking at my clit, and talking wasn't an option, let alone reprimanding.

Leisurely, he wound me up, alternately sucking and licking my swollen bud of nerves while his finger dipped in and out of my hole. Soon it was two fingers, thrusting in farther, rubbing at the sensitive spot inside me, all of it so agonizingly slow that the build in tension felt like hiking up a mountain. I could feel myself getting there, could feel the throb of my pussy increase and my thighs start to shake, could feel my orgasm creeping, creeping toward the summit.

Just when I thought I'd go over, he pulled back. "I thought I'd imagined how good your pussy tasted. But I did not."

"I think that's a compliment, so thank you. Could you go back to tasting now?"

He chuckled as I bucked my hips up toward his mouth, but he did as I asked and went back to work. It was practically starting over now. The brief interruption had sent me back to ground zero. Fortunately, he lapped at me more eagerly this time, helping the tension build quicker.

But just as before, right when I was about to go over the top, he paused to look up at me. And with a grin that said his torture was purposeful.

"What are you doing?" I could hear the frantic edge to my voice.

In comparison, his was casual. "Teasing you."

He blew softly across my wet pussy, sending a round of shocks through my body. I couldn't take it. It was too much. Or it was not enough. It was too much not enough.

I pushed out of his arms and scrambled to my feet and headed toward his bedroom, picking up the shoes I'd kicked off earlier on my way. A few steps away from the door, I paused to reach behind me and unzip my dress, giving him a nice view of my ass. I peeked my head over my shoulder to be sure he was watching.

He was.

"What are you doing?" he asked, an edge in his tone now.

"Teasing *you*," I said, then pushed open the sliding door of his bedroom that had been hidden behind the blackout curtains the last time I'd been there, and stepped inside.

He must have run because he was right behind me when I turned around. Dropping my shoes, I threw my arms around his neck and brought his mouth to mine. His hands circled around my waist and slipped past the open zipper of my dress. Grabbing my ass, he brought me flush against him so I could feel the jutting column of steel flesh against my belly.

I was ready to have that inside me. More than ready. His attention below had left my pussy aching and empty and desperate to be filled with the real thing.

But as eager as I was to have him pushing inside of me, I suddenly realized *I* was dying to see *him*. I'd become acquainted with his cock, not just from the times he'd fucked my pussy, but also from the time he'd fucked my mouth, but except for the one glimpse I'd gotten when I tried to sneak out of his apartment the first time, I was still a stranger to the rest of the body that he kept hidden under well-fitted suits.

Intending to remedy that, I began working at the buttons of his shirt. I'd only managed to pop a couple of them open before he grabbed my hands to stop me.

"I want to see you." Desperation made it sound close to a whine.

He kissed me, as if that would appease the desire to see and touch and lick and claim. "You will. But I was such a good boy the last time you were here, I think I deserve to see you first."

I wasn't sure that was very logical. He'd peeked, and I hadn't gotten to see him at all. Shouldn't it be my turn to see some goods? It seemed only fair.

On the other hand, the way he was looking at me—like he was barely restraining himself, like he was going to eat me up whether I obeyed him or not—made me abruptly lose all care for what was fair.

"If you want to see so badly, I suppose I better show you." I nudged him toward the bed. "Sit."

He seemed maybe not so interested in letting me run things, but he did as I said, undoing the buttons at his cuffs as he sat. "I'm waiting."

I took a step back so he would be able to see all of me clearly, then I pushed one strap off my shoulder than the other, letting my dress fall to the floor. Leaving me completely naked.

It was only after I'd made such a deal of stripping that I remembered I wasn't this bold of a person. I certainly wasn't this confident in my body. Especially being completely nude.

But Scott Sebastian had a way of making me feel wanted, no change necessary, exactly as I was.

Obviously "exactly as I was" wasn't the person Scott assumed I was, but I wasn't going to dwell on that bit at the moment.

Instead, I focused on his gaze, full of hunger as naked as I was. His eyes took their time, moving over every inch of my body, lingering at the tips of my breasts, at the swell of my hips, at the curve of my thighs.

He cleared his throat. "That was worth waiting for." His voice was gruff as he stroked his palm across the bulge in his pants. "Come here."

I walked into the opening between his knees. His hands gripped my hips and brought me closer so he could bury his face in my breasts. "I could suck these all night."

"As long as you're naked when you do, I don't see any problem with it."

He was too busy touching and licking and exploring to respond, and when he did talk, it was to praise and compliment and speak dirty about my body.

So I took it upon myself to get him undressed.

While he bit along the bottom of my breast, I went back to unbuttoning his shirt. Surprisingly, he cooperated, relinquishing his hold on me with one hand at a time so he could pull his arms out. The shirt fell open on the bed, revealing glimpses of hard planes and toned muscles. It was hard to get the view I wanted when he was still so committed to adoring me.

I decided on another tactic. "I need this inside of me," I said, rubbing his cock through his pants. "Please, Scott. I want you so badly it hurts."

Then I climbed onto his lap, straddling him so that my pussy pressed against his length. I rocked back and forth, the feel of his heat and his hardness distracting me from my desire to see him naked. I really did need him inside of me. It really did hurt.

On my next rock back, his hands shot to my waist and stopped me. I followed his gaze down to the wet spot I'd left on his pants. "Look what you did. Fuck, Tessa, that's hot."

Uh, yeah. It was really, really fucking hot.

Abruptly, he flipped me off his lap and to the bed. I scurried higher up the mattress, keeping my eyes pinned on him while he toed off his shoes and took off his pants and boxer briefs at the same time.

Then he stood there. He stood there, cock in hand, pumping it back and forth while he once again devoured me with his gaze.

And finally, I devoured him as well.

God, he was a work of art. He couldn't be any more perfect if he'd been chiseled out of clay. His chest was immaculately sculpted. He had that V-thing going on at his hips, and I'd never fully comprehended what a six-pack was until seeing it now. His legs weren't to be outdone. He was long and lean, his thighs strong and toned. He obviously worked out. And ate well. Two things I barely ever took the time to incorporate in my life, which made me feel a little guilty in the moment, but mostly really damn lucky. And he wasn't bodybuilder fit with muscles that looked like they were trying too hard. They looked more like muscles earned from living an active life.

Considering that I knew Scott spent most of his day behind a desk, he'd definitely had to hit the gym to get the look. Whoever his trainer was, I hoped he was paid well because holy shit he deserved it.

Which took me back to feeling guilty because I didn't deserve it. I'd lied to him—hadn't I? I'd at least outright omitted information about my position at Conscience Connect. I'd let him believe I had authority that I did not have. I didn't deserve this good thing. I didn't deserve to see his glorious body. I didn't deserve to get pleasure from that fantastic cock. I didn't deserve to have my panties in his collection, a collection full of only my panties, nobody else's, if that were to be believed, and of course like the fucking idiot that I was, I stupidly believed.

Deserve it or not, I was here, and I wasn't about to walk out.

No, what I was about to be was fucked.

While I'd been ogling, Scott had dug a condom from his bedside table and had ripped it open with his teeth. Without moving his eyes from me, he unrolled it over his cock. "You ready for me, Tessa? Ready to be fucked in a bed?"

I was definitely ready for the fucking.

But I didn't think I was ready for him at all. Wasn't ready for any of the ways Scott Sebastian was changing me or for any of the feelings he was making me feel.

Since he didn't care about what was going on in my head, and definitely not what was going on in my heart, I answered with, "Yes. I'm ready."

Being fucked in a bed by Scott wasn't a whole lot different than being fucked in his office or in his conference room. And it was completely different at the same time. He still felt the same inside me. He still moved at a punishing pace. He still spoke dirty words as he split me apart with his masterful cock.

But he also gave more attention to the previously neglected parts of my anatomy. His hands and mouth were all over me. And while his thrusts came fast, the entirety of the act was not fast at all. The man had stamina, and he knew how to move himself—how to move me—so that he hit new places inside of me, some that I hadn't known existed before.

He was also more occupied with my reactions than he had been during our quickies. More focused on how I felt. He'd always made me come, of course, but this was more than about just orgasm.

"How do I feel right there?" he'd ask now. "How does this feel like that? Does it make you feel good? Does this make you feel better?"

His questions weren't just concerned with how his cock was hitting me but how other things felt as well. He wanted to know if I preferred sucking or nipping on my breast. If it felt good when he pinched my clit. If I liked it when he spanked my ass. As though he were learning me for later. As though he intended this to go on.

That wasn't the way sex had been with players in the past. *Live in the moment* was the usual motto. *Feel good now.* No reason to discover a person's preference if you weren't planning to fuck them for very long.

This man...This man was doing a real number on my

head.

Countless orgasms later, including two for Scott, I collapsed on the bed while he disappeared to the bathroom to clean up. I was boneless and wrought out. I swore every muscle in my body had been used. If I closed my eyes, I knew I'd be asleep in a heartbeat.

Staying awake meant my brain was awake. With the euphoria wearing off and the lust sated, I began to think things I shouldn't think. Began attaching meaning where there was likely none. Clearly, Scott wanted me as much as I wanted him. The chemistry was undeniable, but was it possible there could be more? Did he want there to be more? *Was* there already more?

He came back from the bathroom with a washcloth and very gently cleaned me up, another gesture that had me fluttering with the possibility of *more*. This was the act of a lover, not a player. What did it mean?

When he was finished, he put one knee on the bed and kissed me, then he pulled me to my feet. This was more like it. This was when he'd give me the *I had a good time, now here's money for a cab* speech.

Instead, he wrapped his arms around me. "I'd really like it if you'd stay the night."

"Well, I was half asleep when you yanked me out of the bed."

"So I could get you under the covers before you were out completely."

"Oh." Having reality turn out to be pleasantly different from my expectations was not something I was used to. "Okay. I'll stay."

"Good." He pulled back the comforter and held it up for me to crawl in. Then he turned off the light and slipped in next to me, spooning me from behind.

Now, with the lights off and his arms around me, it was harder to stay grounded. It was harder not to believe I could mean something to him, that I might mean something to him already, beyond a fun thing to do on a Friday night, that was.

"Scott?" I hadn't spoken loudly, but my voice felt big in the darkness. "Why didn't you want to give me the spiel earlier? The *don't get attached, this is all just for fun* spiel?" I really needed to hear it at the moment.

He paused so long that I thought he'd fallen asleep. I was pretty close to slumber myself.

"I think…" he said finally, my eyes startling open. Silence followed. Then, "I really, really like you Tessa Turani."

I stopped worrying right then that I'd lose my heart to the guy.

I realized I already had.

NINETEEN

"You're awake." Scott watched me from the doorway to his bedroom. He wore nothing but a pair of sweats, but if you asked me, he was entirely overdressed.

"Barely." I sat up with a yawn. My body felt like it could use another couple of hours, but my soul felt rested. "Might be doing better if that's coffee you're holding and if you'll let me steal some."

He approached me, his hand outstretched. "It's for you. And here's your phone. It kept buzzing while I was grinding the beans."

I set the phone on the bed next to me without looking at it. The smell of the fresh roasted coffee was all I could think about at the moment. Well, that and the too-perfect-ly-sculpted-to-be-real man sitting on the edge of the bed next to me.

"Just like I like it," I said after taking my first sip. I'd possibly go so far as to say the best cup of coffee I'd ever had, but while it was a damn good blend doctored up to my liking, the "best" part of it might have had more to do with Scott.

"One cream, two sugars. I pay attention."

I was impressed. And flattered. Also a little suspicious. What kind of guy pays attention to a girl's coffee prefer-ence? The kind of guy who knew how to use that informa-tion to do bad deeds, was who. Those were always the men who moved on quickly.

I was feeling too good to be concerned about that at the moment. "I'm surprised. You were always so wrapped up in your phone in those meetings—well, besides the times you were drilling me down. I wondered if you had a *Clash of Clans* addiction."

"Mostly I traded stocks. A little gambling to keep my mind off how much I wanted to strip you naked and lay you out on that conference room table."

So I hadn't been the only one with those fantasies.

The smile I gave him must have told him what I was thinking because he took the cup out of my hand, set it on the nightstand, and leaned in.

I leaned away. "I have morning breath."

"I don't care."

Neither had I when he'd woken me up in the middle of the night for a second round. Nor had I cared when the third round occurred earlier that morning when the sun streamed in the window and he'd gotten up to shut the blackout curtains.

Eh. Fine. I wouldn't care now either.

"You taste like coffee," he said after a kiss that had my blood stirring.

"You taste like pussy."

He smiled against my mouth, then turned his attention to tugging the sheet down to expose my breasts. Then my belly. Then my everything.

I resisted the urge to curl into a ball and hide, and instead fed his hungry gaze by stretching out and giving him a show, my well-used muscles protesting as I did. "You were right when you said I'd know if we'd had sex."

"Is that right?" He ran his tongue around one spired nipple, then crawled down lower.

"I definitely feel fucked."

His cocky grin said that he felt more than pleased about that fact, and considering that he followed up that smile by licking his tongue around the bud between my legs, I had a feeling I was close to being fucked again.

My phone buzzed from the mattress next to us, reminding me of its presence. Honestly, I was surprised it wasn't dead. I picked it up to move it to the nightstand, glancing at it as I did, and then realized I was fucked in a totally different way.

> In the plethora of texts and missed calls from Kendra—her actual cell instead of a restricted number which didn't bode well—one message stood out from the others. I'm on my way home.

"Shit!" My heart pounded as I flipped through the texts one by one that had started at the ungodly hour of seven a.m.

> To my parents' home, I mean.

I need you to meet me there.

Should I book a train for 2 or 5?

I booked the train at 5. Check your email. You can stay the night.

IMPORTANT: I need you to bring one of my purses.

I'll just call to explain which one.

Missed call from Kendra.

It's my red D & G purse. I'll send a pic.

The next text was a picture of the purse snapped from the internet.

I need THAT specific purse.

Text me to know you got this.

Missed call from Kendra.

Missed call from Kendra.

WHERE ARE YOU?

The doorman knocked at my place and you didn't answer. I texted Tey. She said you didn't stay at home. Are you okay?

DO I NEED TO CALL THE POLICE, TESS? WHERE ARE YOU? I'M WOR-RIED.

"Shit, shit, shit, shit, SHIT."

Scott peered up at me from between my legs. "That wasn't quite the reaction I was going for."

I was crafting a reply, so quickly that I'd already had to start over twice. "Sorry," I said. "I have to go. Like…" I paused my typing to look at the time. Almost half past eleven. *Shiiiiitttt!*

And I had only eleven percent battery left.

"Now. I have to go, like now."

Just woke up. I'll call you in ten. I read over the reply quickly before sending it then threw it on the nightstand and scrambled out of bed to find my dress. And my shoes.

Correction, Kendra's dress and shoes.

Fuck. I was fucked. At least she wasn't already back in the city, but chances were pretty good she'd want to return to NYC with me tomorrow, and I wasn't ready. There were dirty dishes in her sink. I needed to straighten her apartment and pick up the dry cleaning.

Shit!

I had no clean clothes at her house since I'd been borrowing hers, which meant I had to stop by my place in Jersey City to pack an overnight bag.

Then, fuck again!

I had to figure out how to tell her about the deal with SIC. And since I was probably going to get fired after that, I should make sure I didn't leave anything at her apartment that I wouldn't be upset about losing forever. All before catching a train at five.

I had the dress on and zipped and had found one sandal, but the other eluded me. I picked up the comforter we'd thrown to the floor sometime in the night. Not there. Looked under Scott's shirt. His pants. "Have you seen my shoe?" A gleam of gold stuck out from under the curtains. "There it is!"

"Is running out in the morning a pattern with you? It's Saturday, so I know it's not church."

Fuck. Scott.

And not in the good way, but in the I have-to-deal-with-him-too way. When I very much wanted to be *doing* rather than *dealing*.

I could always ignore Kendra. I could stay and spend the day in Scott's bed. I could tell her my phone was dead. If she fired me, well. She was probably going to fire me anyway.

But there was the DRF. And the contracts hadn't been signed. If I wanted the deal to go through, my best chance was to get on Kendra's good side.

I slipped on a sandal and turned back to Scott, sitting on the edge of his bed, looking at me with those blues eyes, and I had all the feels, and there was a good possibility that things between us would blow up soon, so despite my time crunch, I put on my other shoe and made my way over to stand between his legs.

I ran my fingers through his beard. "No. Not a pattern. I'm sorry. It's…" I stopped myself before I said my boss. "A work thing. Another client. Something's come up, and I have to get on it immediately."

He wrapped his hands around my thighs and pulled me in closer so he could nuzzle his head between my breasts. "Immediately, immediately?"

Oh, whoa. He was doing that teasy thing he did with his mouth that made the fabric of my dress rub against my nipple in the most divine way. Which made my pussy start to clench and my thighs tingle and my clit pulse.

The train wasn't until five. I could spare a few minutes, right?

"Well…" My phone buzzed on the nightstand. Probably Kendra's reply. And shit. I'd said I'd call in ten. "Yes.

I have to go immediately. I'm sorry. Really sorry." Sorry for so many things, actually. Like lying about my position and what I was to Kendra and for dropping the guard around my heart.

With a disappointed frown, he ended the breast torture but still kept his arms wrapped tight around me. "At least tell me when I can see you again."

After the truth came to light, he wouldn't want to see me.

Or...maybe he still would? If I came clean before it exploded in my face. Maybe he'd understand. Maybe I could actually hold on to him. Not that a woman could ever hold on to a player forever, but for a little while longer at least.

"Tomorrow night?" I should be able to get away from Kendra by then.

He seemed appeased. More than appeased. Delighted, even. "I can make reservations somewhere."

My stomach flipped. I couldn't bear the idea of being dumped in a five-star restaurant. Not that we were together enough to be dumped. Whatever. I much preferred to do my truth bearing in private.

"You know, I'm perfectly happy with another evening spent here. I'm easy." I leaned into the innuendo, hoping it distracted him from any signs of my anxiety.

"Ooh. I like the sound of that. I could spread you out naked on my dining room table, and I could feed you sushi while I feed on you."

"You wouldn't even have to have the sushi."

"Have I mentioned lately that you're perfect?"

"Not in the last hour." I pressed my mouth to his, slipping my tongue between his lips when I had no business rousing him up like that. Or me. But kissing him was like a drug, and once I started…

My phone buzzed again.

Fuck. "I really have to go. I'm sorry."

Pulling away was hard, and I suddenly understood why Cinderella had lingered so long before running out of the ball. I related to her—a peasant in disguise, parading around in a world I didn't belong in. She'd had to run away. That was the only reason she'd finally been able to make her feet move when she'd so badly wanted to stay.

Her prince had found her. Mine had too, the first time, without even having a shoe.

Her prince hadn't cared who she was in the end.

Would mine?

TWENTY

"Thank God," Kendra exclaimed when I called her on the way to the elevator. "You were really beginning to freak me out!"

It was a thoughtful gesture, worrying about the friend who hadn't come home, but I was a hundred percent convinced she was only freaking out because my absence would have been an inconvenience to her.

"Sorry. I slept in and forgot to plug my phone in last night. I'm only at ten percent right now, so if I lose you, that's why."

"I'll say you slept in. It's almost noon."

I really didn't need her judging me at the moment. "So the five o'clock train?"

"Yes. Did you get the ticket?"

I moved the phone away from my face so I could check my email. "Yep."

"And you have my parents' address?"

Of course I had their fucking address. I was her assistant. I had all the important deets. Not to mention, I knew her parents. I sent them an annual Christmas card. I'd been to the house myself on several occasions.

"Yep." I bit back the real response I wanted to give. "I'll be there with an overnight bag and your purse. Anything else?"

"Nope. But make sure it's the right purse. The one I sent a picture of."

"Got it."

"Can you take a picture of it so I know you have the right one?"

Oh, for fuck's sake. Did she trust me with nothing?

She wouldn't let it drop until she saw the purse, I knew that from experience. I wasn't going to admit that I wasn't currently at her house, not after I'd suggested I'd just woken up there. Fortunately, I'd just stepped in the elevator, and the call dropped.

Good. I'd pretend my battery died and send her a pic when I got to her apartment.

As soon as I was out of the elevator, though, I called Tey.

"Help!" I said in lieu of a greeting.

"I got the text from Kendra, so I figured shit is up. Spill it."

I went outside and hailed a cab while I caught her up, grateful that the clouds overhead hadn't burst because getting a cab was impossible in the rain, and I was not wearing appropriate attire.

Safe in the car on the way to Kendra's apartment, I should have felt calmer, but instead I only felt worse about everything. "It's all going to crumble down, Tey. It's a house of cards, and Kendra's going to find out, and Scott's going to hate me, and the DRF won't be chosen for sponsorship, and Sarah won't give me a job, and Scott is defi-nitely going to hate me."

"You already mentioned the last one."

"It's important enough to mention twice. Were you not listening when I said last night was fucking incredible? And he likes me. He said he likes me! He doesn't mean it, does he? It's just a line, isn't it? I'm being played, aren't I?"

Yeah, I was beginning to unravel.

"Calm your tits, girl, and breathe." She was best-friend-good at pulling me together. Even though I was usually the one coaching Teyana through POTS-induced panic attacks, she'd had her fair share of talking me down as well, which was embarrassing considering how my anxiety was most often centered around a stupid-hot boy.

"Okay. I'm breathing," I said in between breaths.

"Now listen to me. Sure. He might be playing you. I saw the way he looked at you that night at the opera though, and the character he displayed did not seem likely to say shit like that if it wasn't true.

"But this is not the time to figure that all out. Now is the time to focus on Kendra, and I know she can be a bitch of a woman to deal with, but she's also a genuinely kind-hearted person who means well, and I would bet money she'll understand if you are honest and upfront. Focus on that tonight. Tomorrow deal with the boy."

Right. Right. That had to be the plan.

"Did you just say nice things about Kendra?"

"I did. Don't tell anyone. And I mean them. She's not an asshole. And she's going to care about making things right with the DRF, which means honoring whatever you've already started, and she cares about you. So she's going to be hurt, but she's not going to kick you to the curb."

Something in my gut said that Teyana was probably right. She'd spent so much time hating on Kendra—*we'd* spent so much time hating on Kendra—that I'd convinced myself she was worse than she was. "She really does care about us, doesn't she? Why do we rag on her so much?"

"Because we're jealous, and she's privileged, and she hurts us a lot more than she realizes or means to. And because it's what girls do."

I felt bad about that. Mostly I felt bad that in all of this going behind her back, I hadn't considered she'd be hurt by it. Probably because considering it meant that I'd feel the way I did now. Like shit.

"Remember you were trying to do something good for the DRF," Tey went on, seeming to sense my self-loathing over the mobile network and wanting to make me feel better.

Actually, I'd been just as focused on doing something good for myself. But thinking about that right now only made me feel worse, so I dismissed that bit of truth from my mind.

"That's why I have to pull this off. For them." For Tey. "And you will. Do you want me to come with you to Greenwich? For moral support?"

Yes. "No. I'd never put you through that."

"You're running short of time, though. I could pack a

bag for you and meet you at Kendra's and help clean."

"No fucking way are you cleaning her house."

"I'll meet you at Grand Central then."

"You'd be down for the rest of the weekend after that kind of excursion."

"I'd do it for you!"

"I know, and I'm not letting you." Especially if I wouldn't be there to help take care of her afterward.

She gave a frustrated sigh. "Then I'll have your bag packed for you so it can be a quick in and out."

That I'd accept. "Thank you, Tey. For always being there when I need you."

"Only giving back what you give me."

"Love you, and see you soon."

I rushed like a locomotive once I got to Kendra's. I hung up the dress I was currently wearing in her closet, hoping it smelled fresh—I really hadn't worn it long—and changed into a pair of yoga pants and a T-shirt of mine that was overdue for a wash. Then I plugged in my phone, gathered dirty dishes from around the house, and stuck them in the dishwasher without a rinse first. It probably wasn't good enough, but it would have to do. The rest of the place didn't look as bad as I'd remembered since the housekeeper had been there the day before. Her closet required the most work as I tried to arrange things as close to how she left them as possible. I gave up after spending too much time on it, deciding I'd tell her that I'd had to hunt for the purse she'd wanted since that was true.

After that, I picked up the dry cleaning and dropped it back off at her house, collected my bag of laundry and phone and her damn red purse, and splurged on a cab to Jersey City since taking the city transportation would have required both a subway and a bus trip and even if it rained, going by car would shave off thirty minutes.

As promised, Tey met me at the door, handing over a packed overnight bag and a battery pack in exchange for my dirty laundry. "Do you have time for a shower?" she asked.

I didn't really, but I smelled like sex and Scott, both fragrances I didn't mind holding on to in other circumstances, and there was no way I was fit to be present in front of any of the Montgomerys in my current state.

"I'll make it quick."

Twenty minutes later, with wet hair and a sandwich Tey had thrown together for me while I'd showered, I got in another cab and headed to Grand Central station.

I made my train just as they called for final boarding.

It was an hour ride to Connecticut. Not too long, but long enough to get myself together and decide what I was going to say to Kendra. Stupidly, I didn't do either and ended up spending most of the time googling Scott Sebastian. Something I should have done ages ago because the search results that came up were a definite reminder of who I was dealing with. Image after image after image of Scott looking all suave and devastating, a different gorgeous girl on his arm each time. Some pics were posed for the camera at formal events. Some were candid. Then I found a paparazzi shot with him and a woman on the couch/bed on his balcony. It wasn't close up, but her head was in his lap and it was obvious what she was doing.

I studied each one, waiting to feel the stab of jealousy that I usually felt when I saw a man I liked with women more beautiful than me. It didn't come like I'd expected, though. I was too high from waking up in his bed to be brought down. Too high off the fact that I'd seen him last night and was seeing him again tomorrow when none of the other women he was posted with were seen with him twice.

That didn't mean anything, I knew. What was captured in pictures was only a splice of real life. I hadn't had any pictures (to my knowledge) with the man, after all. But it was a gut feeling, an instinct to believe I was special that was probably way off base and totally made up, and even knowing that in my head, my heart chose to believe there might actually be something real.

Was that the most crazy thing in the world?

Then I came across the one image that did jab at me— one with Scott and Kendra. It was a group shot, and I wasn't even sure she and he were a couple in it, but she was at his side, and though the smile on his face didn't hit his eyes, hers looked genuine. It was only one picture, taken at a huge charity event sponsored by the Montgomerys. There were so many reasons that Kendra could be happy in the picture that had nothing to do with Scott Sebastian.

But there was an unsettled ache between my ribs at the possibility that it was. Was that why she hadn't wanted to pitch to the Sebastians? Because she'd been pining over one of Henry's sons? If so, did she like him enough to ruin a potential partnership if she discovered I'd slept with him?

It was pointless trying to guess. And my imagination was wild and overactive, and chances were I was reading far too much into one little smile.

It was raining when I got to Greenwich, which meant waiting for an Uber. By the time I got to Kendra's parents' thirteen-thousand-square-foot home in the suburbs, it was nearly seven.

She jumped on me the minute the butler let me in the door—yes, the Montgomerys had a real live butler. "You're here, you're here, you're here!" She threw her arms around me, seeming not to care that I was wet from rain, and she was dressed up—and not in an outfit that matched the red purse if you asked me, but I wasn't the fashion guru she was. "Thank you for coming. You saved my ass. Again. What would I do without you?"

She didn't give me time to respond before going on. "Did you bring the purse?"

"Yeah, yeah." I maneuvered my overnight bag on my shoulder so I could dig inside. I'd thrown it in there to be sure it stayed safe since, obviously, it was important. "Here you go."

"Ah! Thank you!" She opened the bag and rummaged in an inside pocket, pulling out a ring and placing it on her finger.

Oh. It had been about jewelry, not the bag itself. Equally as frivolous. Figured.

Before I could think more about it, she looked me over and made a fretful sort of noise.

"Are you wearing that?"

I glanced down at the not-too-casual maxi dress I'd

thrown on when I'd gotten out of the shower. "...yes? Was I supposed to be wearing something different?"

She sighed—at herself, not at me. "I should have told you tonight was fancy. You can borrow something from my closet upstairs."

She hadn't told me there was a "tonight" that I was a part of at all. My impression had been that I was delivering a purse for whatever plans she had with her family, and I'd hide away in one of the many guest bedrooms and Netflix and chill with myself for the night.

Like, literally since I had my pocket vibrator with me and thoughts of Scott were at the forefront of my mind.

Looking around for the first time, I realized that the family plans were more than family plans. There was a banquet table set out in the great room behind her, caterers flitting around setting it up. Leila Montgomery, Kendra's mother, was dressed in a cocktail dress speaking very preparing-to-be-a-hostess-like to someone wearing a chef's hat. And a glance out the window by the door to the circle drive showed a car sitting there with fancy-dressed people getting out of the back seat and more cars pulling up.

"Seriously? There's a party?" I'd been to parties at the Montgomerys' before. They were exhausting events that tended to spiral Kendra into a tizzy, and not because her parents were elitist aristocrats but because their guests tended to be. Very many of those guests were also potential Kendra clients. No wonder she'd been concerned with looking just right.

"Not a party," she assured me. "Spur-of-the-moment gathering. My parents threw something together this morning when they heard I was coming."

It seemed the whole world dropped at the snap of Kendra's fingers. Including me. Was she to blame for that or those around her?

Well, it wasn't going to be my fault this time. "I'm not intruding on your party. I'm tired and ready for bed. No one will miss me if I spend the evening in the guest room."

"That's crazy! The buffet Mom ordered is spectacular."

"I'll sneak something from the kitchen."

"Terese Turani, stop being such a recluse." Said the woman who'd run away to introvert for the last two and a half weeks. "Be with me. I've missed you!"

It was that same sincere smile I'd seen in the picture with Scott. A smile I was well familiar with, as I was with all her smiles, having known her so well for so many years now. It was a smile that told me she meant it, that she missed me. That she wanted me to be there. It reminded me why I did love her, despite all the resentment I had for her. Because she was full of life and infectious energy and as much as she drained me, she also filled me back up.

"Okay. Okay." The doorbell rang behind me. "I'd better go up and get presentable."

She waited for me to disappear up the stairs before opening the door, thank goodness, because while I'd dressed appropriately for a quiet night with the Montgomerys, I did not look good enough for their company.

After dropping my bag off in the room that was always given to me on my visits, I headed to Kendra's room and chose a simple black sheath dress, something both elegant enough to seem like I belonged yet plain enough that I could disappear. It was funny that here I was wearing her clothes once again. I shouldn't have even bothered packing my own bag.

I was glad I'd gotten the chance to shower though. While my hair wasn't in any shape to leave down, it was clean and easy to throw it into a knot. Kendra and I didn't have quite the same shade of skin tone so I couldn't borrow much of her makeup, but I rummaged through her drawers anyway and found a blush that worked and used her mascara and put on some lipstick I'd brought of my own.

Almost thirty minutes later, I came back down to find the party—no way was this only a *gathering*—in full swing. Granted, it wasn't crowded like the Montgomerys' usual events that hosted up to two hundred people, but those always extended into the yard so even the fifty or, so people I guessed were there felt crowded with everyone confined indoors.

The good news was that it was enough people that I'd be able to sneak away as soon as I made an appearance. Now to find Kendra.

I lingered at the bottom of the stairs, looking over the sea of faces for hers while I tried to remember what she'd been wearing.

I was found before I found her. "Tess, you made it! Glad to see you. I know how important it was for Kendra to have you here tonight." Leila pulled me into an embrace, reminding me how good she was at hugging. "Is your room okay?"

I tended to forget that in the time between visits. It was easy to lump her in with all the other well-off people we dealt with at Conscience Connect, and I often found my-self thinking of her as an out-of-touch socialite when really she was a very generous and warm woman. Because she had money, I wanted to think of her as selfish and materi-alistic, but she was nothing of the sort. She'd dedicated her life to philanthropy, for God's sake. She'd raised a daugh-ter who had built a career that helped fund charitable orga-nizations. She had the gift of service in her blood, and she gave damn good hugs.

"The room is perfect, as always."

"Good. I'm relieved. I haven't really used it since the last time you were here, and we have some other guests staying tonight, so I didn't have anywhere to move you if there was a problem. You know where to find extra bed-ding if you need it?"

"Yep. I remember."

"Of course you do." She looked me over, and not in the are-you-appropriately-dressed look over way, but in the I'm-genuinely-interested sort of way. "You look fantastic, by the way. Did you do something different to your hair?"

The only thing I'd done different since I'd last seen her was betray her daughter and fuck Scott Sebastian. And if I looked fantastic, it was because I was wearing her daughter's clothes. "I think I've gained five pounds?"

"It looks amazing on you. Make sure to hit the dessert bar and gain five more."

"I'll do that." Sincerely, I would. She always chose the best caterers, and after all this socializing, I was going to need an ostentatious chocolatey thing of some sort. "Do you know where I can find—?"

Before I could finish, Kendra was at my side, grabbing my hand like we were teenage girls instead of women near thirty. "Nice choice!" she exclaimed, remarking over my dress. "I should have told you to get into my jewelry. That would look perfect with my diamond pendant choker."

With barely a breath in between, she returned a wave to someone across the room. "I need to catch up with you, Kay. Later. After you eat something."

Then her attention was back to me. "Thank God you came. I've gotten so used to anti-peopling, I don't remember how to people. Tell me how to people, will you?" Again, her eye caught elsewhere. "Janet! Look at your baby bump! Three months to go now?"

"Thirteen weeks," Janet replied, as though that extra week definitely needed to be accounted for. "Too long."

"It will go by in a heartbeat." It seemed like Kendra was peopling just fine to me.

But I knew this was the sort of socializing that exhausted her. "Keep up exactly what you're doing. Then, when it's all over, you'll take some hot cocoa upstairs and soak in the tub with *Outlander* on the TV."

She closed her eyes and made a delicious sound like she was already imagining it. "I really do love *Outlander*. And hot cocoa. And soaking in tubs."

"I know you do, K."

Her gaze was somewhere else now. "Bruce and Cathy! Good to see you!"

"You too. Congratulations," one of them said. Bruce, I was guessing, since it was a male voice.

"Thank you!" She threaded her arm through mine.

"Make the rounds with me, will you?" she asked, already pulling me along with her into the crowd.

"Yep." But something was itching at me all of a sudden. "Are we...celebrating something?"

She mouthed a hello and waved at yet another guest across the room, and this time I really looked at the ring she'd retrieved from the red purse. Really thought about it and why she was wearing it on her left hand. "K, that looks an awful lot like an engagement ring."

"Oh, yeah," she sighed like whatever story she was about to tell was a drag. "I should have told you already, but I just didn't know—ah! There you are. Let me introduce you."

I was pretty sure her last couple of sentences weren't meant for me but for the tuxedoed man she'd now broken from me to speak with. "My assistant is here. I want you to meet her."

He had his back to me, and my eye was caught on Kendra's ringed hand, possessively sitting on his shoulder blade. It was quite a ring. Three carats? Four?

Then I really looked at the man's backside. Most men look the same in a tux, and this one was no different, but the build was familiar. And the length and style of his hair. And was that a hickey peeking up over the collar of his jacket?

I knew that hickey. I'd made that hickey.

Panic and dread and utter shock swamped over me. I wanted to run. I needed to run, but my feet were glued in place as the bearded man pivoted to face me.

To his credit, his expression remained steady as Kendra introduced him. "Tess," she said brightly. "This is Scott Sebastian. My fiancé."

MAN IN LOVE

*Scott and Tess's story concludes in **Man in Love.***

Scott Sebastian is a liar.

Fitting, since I'm a liar too.

Yet there's no place for me in his glittering world of half-truths.

With all our secrets in the open, I should stop trying. What I've learned should send me running far away. I can't keep pining for a man in love if I'm not the woman he's in love with.

But it's not that easy to escape the Sebastians. I already knew they owned this city.

Now I'll find out if they also own their son.

Join my reader group, **The Sky Launch**.

Follow me on **Bookbub** and **Instagram**.

Like my author page.

Sign up for my newsletter where you'll receive a **free book every month** from bestselling authors, only available to my subscribers, as well as up-to-date information on my latest releases.

Visit **www.laurelinpaige.com** to find out more about me and all my books.

ABOUT THE AUTHOR

With millions of books sold, Laurelin Paige is the NY Times, Wall Street Journal, and USA Today Bestselling Author of the Fixed Trilogy. She's a sucker for a good romance and gets giddy anytime there's kissing, much to the embarrassment of her three daughters. Her husband doesn't seem to complain, however. When she isn't reading or writing sexy stories, she's probably singing, watching shows like Killing Eve, Letterkenny and Discovery of Witches, or dreaming of Michael Fassbender. She's also a proud member of Mensa International though she doesn't do anything with the organization except use it as material for her bio.

www.laurelinpaige.com
laurelinpaigeauthor@gmail.com

9 781953 520012